Rails on the Wind

Rails on the Wind

Philip Gulick

Northwest Publishing, Inc.
Salt Lake City, Utah

Rails on the Wind

This is a work of fiction.
All characters and events portrayed in this book are fictional,
and any resemblance to real people or incidents is purely coincidental.

For information address: Northwest Publishing, Inc.
6906 South 300 West, Salt Lake City, Utah 84047
ESH 01 19 95
Edited by C. Gleason

PRINTING HISTORY
First Printing 1995

ISBN: 1-56901-442-6

NPI books are published by Northwest Publishing, Incorporated,
6906 South 300 West, Salt Lake City, Utah 84047.
The name "NPI" and the "NPI" logo are trademarks belonging to
Northwest Publishing, Incorporated.

PRINTED IN THE UNITED STATES OF AMERICA.
10 9 8 7 6 5 4 3 2 1

This novel is dedicated to my mother, Jean Frances Cooper, who gave me the West, and to my wife, Barbara, whose common sense kept my dreams from becoming nightmares.

Preface

This is a fictional account of the Burlington & Missouri River Railroad and the people who built it from Crawford, Nebraska, to Billings, Montana, at the turn of the century.

Many of the characters depicted were or are real. Others are pure fiction. Although the story authentically depicts the construction of the railroad, its route and the towns along the right-of-way, it is not intended as an official history of the Burlington Railroad.

I have attempted to follow as closely as possible the historic events depicted, but other events are pure fiction.

For my pen name, I have used my mother, Jean Frances Cooper's name, and my stepfather Joseph Gulick's name, since I owe so much to both of them.

I assume full responsibility for any errata, misconceptions, or misrepresentations in this novel.

Introduction

My grandfather, George Sanford Cooper, is buried in Custer, Montana, not far from the Little Big Horn River and the Custer Battlefield.

George Sanford Cooper was eleven years old and living in Georgetown, Ohio, when the Battle of the Little Big Horn was fought on that bright spring day of June 25, 1876.

It wasn't until nearly thirteen years later that Cooper made his first acquaintance with the Great West as a telegraph operator for the Chicago, Burlington & Quincy Railroad. He had qualified at Sardenia, Ohio, and stepped aboard a train bound for Omaha, Nebraska, his first venture away from the hard life as a sharecropper on his family's Feesburg, Ohio farm.

Thirty-one hard years were to follow before George Sanford

Cooper was laid to rest in Custer. During his life, Cooper married an aristocratic English woman, fathered ten children and reared them on his meager railroad salary in some of the Western Frontier's wildest towns. One of his daughters was my mother, born in Ranchester, Wyoming, and buried in Denver.

Cooper was not a perfect father nor perfect worker, as my mother's extensive family journal reveals. He was forever burdened by his wife's constant social climbing, the wild scramblings of his children and the demands of his job. He was one of thousands of railroad men driving steel rails through uncharted, untamed and mostly unpopulated land.

U. S. Interstate Highway 90 now cuts a four-lane swath acrossWyoming, from Beulah on the South Dakota border west and north to Sheridan near the Montana border.

Although sixteenth-century Spanish and European explorers rarely ventured into what was Unorganized Territory, as early as 1811, the John Jacob Astor's Astorians had explored what is today the state of Wyoming.

Astor and his Pacific Fur Company men, Wilson Price Hunt, Robert Stuart and notably Donald McKenzie, made fur-seeking expeditions into Wyoming in the early 1800s.

More impressive were the wide-ranging excursions of Jedediah S. Smith, the most remarkable explorer of the West. Smith was the first to discover the natural gateway to the Oregon country, the first white overland explorer to reach California and the first to cross the Sierra Nevada.

Smith's summer excursions of 1822 and 1825 from the Missouri River in South Dakota almost parallel today's Interstate 90. Federal wagon-roads cut by the U. S. Army from 1849–1869, to supply its far-flung western forts, in some degree also parallel Interstate 90.

Today, Interstate 90 cuts across some of the country's most famous and historic trails.

The Texas Cattle Trail of 1840–1897 cuts northward through Lusk, Wyoming, into Miles City, Montana, and across the Canadian border. At one point, it was called the Montana Trail.

Probably the most famous, the Oregon Trail, bent off west from Fort Laramie to South Pass, more closely following the route of today's Interstate 25.

The Overland Mail and Express routes made it as far north as Casper, Wyoming, and today's Interstate 90 does not cut those trails. The Pony Express routes also more parallel Interstate 25 than they do Interstate 90.

Stagecoach routes from 1847–1881 mostly followed old, established trails. Interstate 90 crosses just northeast of the most famous and romantic of them all, the Deadwood-Cheyenne Stagecoach Line. Another more arduous route ran from Julesburg, Colorado, northwest across Wyoming to Virginia City, Montana. Interstates 25 and 90 both cross that route.

Then came the railroads.

Early construction of America's transcontinental railroads bypassed Wyoming Territory for political and financial reasons. However, it wasn't long before far-sighted men saw the great potential of the West's natural resources in timber, beaver, buffalo and vast expanses for new farmers and ranchers.The first railroad to penetrate Wyoming Territory was the Burlington, formed in 1849 as the Chicago, Burlington & Quincy Railroad. It became the Burlington Route in 1855 and slowly expanded west and north by construction and the purchase of 203 smaller roads.

The Burlington played a key role in the development of the Midwest, especially Nebraska, Wyoming and Montana. Today's Burlington Northern, a merger of the Burlington, Northern Pacific and Great Northern railroads, is the longest railroad in America with more than 26,000 miles of track. By 1882, the Chicago, Burlington & Quincy Railroad had reached

Denver. In 1884 it began building across Wyoming with branch lines into the Black Hills. By 1894, it had reached a point near Billings, Montana, where, joined with the Northern Pacific, it gained access to the Pacific and the Great Northwest. George Sanford Cooper, his wife and their children poured their blood, sweat and tears into that railroad for nearly forty years.

It is to them, and thousands of other men, women and children, that I dedicate this work. Without them, there would have been no "Golden West." Without them, I wouldn't be here.

Philip Cooper-Gulick, 1995

Rails on the Wind

The Farm

Brag Cooper stood between the rails as the locomotive roared toward him, then leaped aside seconds before it would have ground him to pieces. The engineer laughed as the train thundered past, jetting steam and dust over Brag's hard-muscled young body.

The first time Brag challenged the locomotive, the engineer gave him the finger and shouted a curse as he sped past. It became almost a daily game between them. Then, one day the engineer tossed out a note. "You will make one hell of an engineer some day, boy," it read.

Right then and there, Brag decided the railroad was for him.

The year was 1889 and Brag was trapped by a domineering father and the unrelenting boredom of their farm near

Feesburg, Ohio. He was yearning for an escape.

Brag had returned that morning from Burlington, Iowa, working on the tenant farm owned by his brother-in-law John Berry. He thought it would be a welcome break from his home, but it turned out to be the same tedious routine of the field.

Berry told Brag about the railroads' explosive expansion. New railroads were striking west, carrying thousands of people lured by rich Colorado and California gold strikes. Limitless sections of profitable land were being bought and sold along the right of way.

Berry's stories filled Brag's imagination with images of the far-off West. He would be a telegrapher, a conductor, maybe even an engineer. If he could not cut it with the railroad, he'd strike out for the gold camps.

As he watched the train disappear down the valley of trees, Brag just knew his future rode west with it.

Brag kicked at a rail, muscles tingling under his sun-baked skin. He felt his body would explode any second. Sparks from that locomotive had ignited a fuse within him.

He skirted the shallow pond that was the farm's irrigation source and trudged up the path to the farmhouse. It was harvest time and the family would be in the fields until well after dark.

"Where have you been, Brag?" Rebecca asked, shaking the dirt from a string rug.

"Up on the tracks, Mom."

"Sam isn't going to like that," she frowned. "Tough on you, isn't it, Brag? You've got a vagabond in you pounding to get out."

He nodded.

"Well, we are eating supper in a few minutes," she said. "Might as well get cleaned up. I think your father's got some news for you."

He watched her, a thin, fragile woman with blue eyes and auburn hair pulled into a tight bun. Her movements were efficient, cloned by more than thirty years hard in a routine. She had married Sam in 1860, moved into the farm and almost immediately, their brood of nine children started coming.

Now, thirty strenuous years later, birthing, anxiety and death had left her drained and wrinkled.

Sam came around the corner of the house, stamped mud from his boots and glared at Brag.

"Been loafing, again?" he asked, peeling off his boots. His thick, muscled arms glistened with sweat as he brushed the black dust from his grimy beard and dug a pipe from his shirt pocket. "You know it's harvest, boy, and we need every hand. You can't loaf around here."

Sam never spoke to Brag, he issued commands. Brag didn't flinch. He'd been through this a thousand times.

"I just got back from Berry's."

"He paid you then? Where is it?"

Brag dug the bills from his dungarees.

"Not much for you loafing off at Berry's for three days," Sam said, fingering the three dog-eared one dollar bills. Brag was triggered to explode, but said nothing.

"Letter came for you yesterday from Sardinia. I opened it. I'll tell you about it over supper." Privacy, even to personal letters, meant nothing to Sam in a household of curious kids.

A large, finely worked oak table was the Cooper family's center piece, serving at meals, evening prayers, reading and writing, Sam's bookkeeping and Rebecca's sewing.

"Listen," Sam ordered over the chatter of the hungry children, "Mr. Berry's got a job for Brag. The Chicago, Burlington & Quincy Railroad needs telegraph operators out west. Berry arranged it so Brag can take the test tomorrow in Sardinia. We'll have to do without him again during harvest." He glared at Brag.

"That's swell!" Brag exclaimed.

Sam grimaced. "Berry left those Morse Code books for you," Sam growled.

Brag sprawled on the bed and opened the volume. He caught on almost immediately to the dot and dash equivalents for each letter. The noise of the family gathering tools for tomorrow's first light interrupted his study. He had been a part of the harvest since he could remember. Now, he had no regrets. He rolled over and went to sleep, the locomotive whistle echoing in his head.

"Morning, Brag," Berry said as he pulled the twin bay geldings and rig up to the farm the next morning. "Did you get into the books last night?"

"Yes and I can't thank you enough for the chance, Mr. Berry."

"Good. We'd better be going. It's not far to Sardinia, but the road's soft."

The tiny Washington Township village of Sardinia lay eighteen miles northeast of the farm. The narrow rutted road cut through the White Oak River bluffs and climbed to a forested plain. About three-hundred townsfolk lived in Sardinia, nestled on the east branch of White Oak Creek. The Cincinnati & Eastern Railroad passed through the town and it soon would be the terminus of another railroad, the Hillsboro & Sardinia. Two other railroads were considering the routes nearby.

"You know, Brag, the railroads along the Ohio River are finally winning the battle with the steamboats," Berry said. "The railroad offers lower rates, faster and more reliable service and I think the steamboat is on its way out." He clicked at the geldings and they responded, digging eagerly into the soft road.

The morning dew glistened gold in the sunlight and a blue fog hugged the hollows in miniature rainbows.

The geldings followed the familiar twin grooves until they topped the bluff and pulled up to Nathan Dunn's Marshall House in Sardinia where Berry had booked rooms.

"We can have supper with some friends later. My usual poker game, too. You better get in more studying," Berry said.

Brag was clear-headed and primed when he sat down in the Marshall House the next morning with thirty-two, young, would-be telegraphers. Telegraph keys sat on each desk, wired to a sound box at the main desk. Three bearded men moved around the room, instructing each of the neophytes.

"My name is Mr. Farswell," a tall, gaunt man said to the

class. "I'm the chief telegrapher for the Chicago, Burlington & Quincy Railroad out of our headquarters in Lincoln, Nebraska. Now, we have need of good telegraphers in Nebraska, Wyoming and Montana. The Burlington, we call it the Q, is heading west like a runaway locomotive." He laughed at his own simile.

"What we do now is test you for basic aptitude. If you pass, we put you through an intensive week of schooling. If you pass that, we will send you to one of our stations in Nebraska or further west."

Each student answered in code with the key, a word called out by Farswell. He wrote down the response opposite the applicant's name. Each was given ten words to spell in code and graded on accuracy and speed. Brag remembered a picture of the key on the books, but he'd never touched one before. His hands began to sweat as he practiced. He watched with growing satisfaction as the others fumbled with the keys. Right then, he knew he would not be the slowest in the class.

"Pretty good, Cooper," Farswell beamed. "You finished at ten words a minute, well below our standard of twenty or better, of course. However, with practice, you could become a fair telegrapher."

Brag thought, was it going to be that easy?

"The four of you who passed here today can attend our school beginning next Monday," Farswell said. "It cost ten dollars."

No, thought Brag, it wasn't going to be that easy.

Farswell then dismissed them, but took Brag aside. "Is Mr. Berry in town?" he asked.

"Yes, he's downstairs."

"Fine, then please deliver this to him." He scribbled out a note and handed it to Brag.

"Be sure he gets this, and don't read it, Cooper," he commanded.

Brag settled into a chair next to Berry feeling gloomy. He had conquered the first major challenge of his life, but had little hope of attending the school. The ten dollars was more than his family made in a months' hard work.

Berry was smiling, surrounded by three railroad toughs and the station master. He had a drink in one hand, a diamond flush in the other.

"Well, Brag, how did you do?" he inquired, apparently not interested.

"Quite well, I think. Mr. Farswell sent you this. He wanted to know if you were in town."

"That damn scoundrel," Berry laughed. "He wanted to know so he could disappear. He owes me two dollars from our last poker game. Let's see what he has to say." He broke into laughter as he read the note. "He wants me to wait until next month for the money. Hell if I will, he'll see my lawyer first." He laughed.

Brag expected there was something in the note about him.

"Oh, by the way, Brag, he says something about you," Berry said, as an afterthought.

"Play your hand, Berry," commanded one of the toughs.

"Okay, beat a diamond flush!" he roared, slapping down his cards. They cursed as he raked in the five dollar pot.

Finally, he reopened the note. "Says here, Brag, you have the makings of a first-class telegrapher. I always knew you were clever with your hands. I also know how badly you want to get away from the farm and all. Well, perhaps you are on your way."

"It came natural. I was pretty clumsy with the key, but the hard studying paid off," Brag said.

Berry grinned. "Obviously. Well, we will discuss this with your folks. I know it will take some money. We will talk about it later. Right now, have a drink."

Berry said nothing about the school on their journey home, leaving a dejected Brag at the farm with a curt, "So long, see you soon."

Brag told the family about the trip at supper that night, delighting Rebecca and the youngsters.

"You can't go, boy," Sam said after supper. "We'll get a good share if this harvest is fat, but I've got ground rent and we all need new shoes. I don't have the money."

"I know. Maybe I should have gambled like Berry. He won five dollars."

"You were at the Marshall House?" Sam shot back.

"I shouldn't have let on, I guess."

"It's fine with me. About time you grew up some. Don't let Rebecca know, though," Sam demanded. "Did you get drunk?"

"I guess so, I staggered around a bit." Sam did not smile.

Brag cried that night. His dream was as fleeting as the three dollars he gave to Sam. He'd earned that himself and he could have scraped up the other seven dollars somehow.

The corn husks peeled off like paper under Brag's strong hands as he worked out his frustration in the fields the next morning.

Berry came by that afternoon and called Sam and Brag in from the fields. They sat in the barn, smoking and talking as the sun beat down on the corrugated tin roof.

"Sam, I want to send Brag to that telegraphers' school next week," Berry began, showing Farswell's note to Sam.

"Dammit, Mr. Berry, your harvest is going to rot as we speak, but it's your money," Sam exclaimed. "I can't do without a single hand, not if you want your harvest."

"I know that, dammit, Sam," Berry shot back. Sam and Berry had been friends for twenty-five years and disagreement was common.

"Brag's got a chance to better himself. Shit, Sam, you're as bullheaded as ever!"

Sam walked away. Brag stood aside and said nothing.

"Look, Sam, I know you're in a pinch," Berry went on. "I'll send the Claremonts over. Their harvest is already in."

Brag's future brightened, but another blow fell with Berry's next words.

"Brag, I've got a stand of pine a few miles north that needs clearing." He paused, wiped the sweatband of his expensive Derby, then went on. "If you clear half of it, I'll give you the ten dollars. If you clear all of it, I'll give you thirteen dollars. That would be enough for board and room at the hotel and a few extra bucks, too."

"That's a lot of timber," Brag said. He and Sam had cleared their land and Brag still recalled the sting of blistered hands. That was only a few stubborn pitch pines. Berry was talking about a whole stand of them.

"I'll do it," Brag exclaimed. "You don't know how much I want to go to that school."

"Yes, I do," Berry responded with a laugh. He slapped Brag on the back and left.

A week later in Sardinia, the students gathered for more sessions on telegraphy.

"I can handle it, how about you?" Jesse Skowron asked Brag as they fumbled with the keys.

"It's not easy, but I'm getting it," Brag responded.

"I'm struggling right now. Since you are so good at this, maybe you can help me?" Skowron implored, his words whistling through a gap in his front teeth. He was thin as a pine needle, with an unruly shock of bright red hair and freckles dotting his face and arms.

That night in the saloon, Brag threw back more drinks than he could handle to quell the pain of his blistered hands. Their final test was the next morning and Brag needed the tonic that whiskey seemed to supply.

Brag and the other three neophytes studied strange railroad terms: butcher, pie boy, spotters and call boy. Standard Time had to be extrapolated into code and station names. Time tables, routes and the electrical complexities of telegraphy were pounded into their heads.

The four survivors took their seats that Saturday morning and listened to Farswell explain the final testing. They sweated through two full hours of key-tapping and concentrated listening that left them exhausted.

Brag sat on the outside steps with his fellow students, feeling an uneasiness in his stomach. He was sure his accuracy was up to Farswell's standard, but he may have keyed too slowly. He might have failed on speed, but all he could do now was wait.

"How did you do, Jesse?" Brag asked.

"I think okay, how about you?" Skowron replied.

"Too slow, I suspect, but I was pretty accurate, I think," Brag said grimly.

Farswell stuck his head out the door. "You can all return to your seats, gentlemen." He perched on the corner of the desk, dangling one leg in the air.

"All of you passed, and I consider that pretty good," he said. "Before this week is out, you should receive by post your certificates of completion and notification of employment."

He got up, shook each student's hand and smiled. "It's wonderful to work with such bright, young men. I wish you all luck. We probably will meet later down the line. Until then, good-bye and God bless you."

"Well, old chap, we've done it!" Brag shouted as he pumped Skowron's hand.

"Believe me, I've never done anything like this down on the farm," Brag exclaimed. "I wonder where we'll be going?"

"It's the Rocky Mountains for me," Skowron chimed.

"Me, too," Brag affirmed.

"Look out, Marshall's, here we come!" Skowron shouted. They marched proudly into the saloon.

As Brag suspected, Berry was there, a pile of bills attesting to the fact his luck was still holding.

"Well, if it isn't the kiddie corps of key-pounders," Berry laughed. "Pull up a bottle and have a drink on me.

"Well, Brag, tell me about it. Did you hack out a bunch of garbage up there or did you make a grand success of yourself?" asked Berry.

"Top of the class, sir," Brag shot back proudly.

"Excellent, Brag. I expected nothing less. I suspect you'll go west. They're laying rails a mile a minute out there. That calls for a celebration. I'm sure you deserve it."

He ordered several bottles of choice whiskey and raked in the pot.

They partied well into the morning, finally staggering down the street to the hotel where Brag spent a sick, sleepless night. When he awoke, his head full of lightning bolts and mouth full of cotton, he wondered if success deserved such a dubious reward.

Berry let the geldings have their heads on the way home along the bluffs and down into the valley. They knew the way. Brag's head spun like the wheels of the rig and his stomach turned over like a butter churn. Berry stopped several times to let him empty the sour whiskey on the road. The cold morning air soon improved his condition.

He had one good celebration and another would come from a family overjoyed at his success, except Sam. He would finish the harvest while waiting for the letter from the railroad, then he'd be on his way. Oh, life suddenly was so sweet.

The elm and oak trees that hung over the twisting, rutted road had dropped their leaves in bushels. The geldings swirled through them in crackling little tornadoes as they trotted along the high bluffs overlooking the valley. They dropped onto the bottom land and picked up an easy gait straight to the farm.

The family had been in the fields since sunup, cutting low the now naked corn stalks. The Percheron heaved forward easily against the plow as it turned over rich, black clumps of soil. The family shouted with glee and ran to the house when Brag and Berry appeared.

"The prodigal son is back, crowned in glory," cried Rebecca, embracing Brag as he climbed down.

"Yes, mother, I passed! I'm a railroad telegrapher now!" Alfred pumped his hand vigorously and Louetta rained kisses on his cheeks. His brothers and sisters tugged at his clothing for attention. Sam shook his hand without a smile or a word.

"Come on in, Mr. Berry, have a drink," Sam invited.

"Sorry, Sam, I've got to carry Mary Margaret to Cincinnati today," he replied. "Take good care of Brag. See you all soon." He clicked at the bays and they disappeared into the woods.

"Brag, we're almost finished, but we still need you out there," Sam said.

"I'll change and be right out," Brag said. "A bit of sweat

will shake this hangover."

"Shame on you, Brag," admonished Rebecca with mock modesty.

"Yea, we really celebrated. I passed the test, tops in the class." He couldn't wait to relate all that happened to him during the past week.

"I'm so proud of you, Brag," Rebecca cried. "That means you'll be leaving us soon, doesn't it?" Brag saw the hurt in her eyes.

"I think so, Mother, when the letter comes. I'll know later this week. Probably some station out west."

"Okay, enough of this, let's get to the harvest," Sam said.

They finished the last field after dark while Rebecca was preparing a special meal. She served the cured ham that had been hanging in the smokehouse, sweet yams, green beans, ears of golden corn and plump tomatoes. She topped it with crisp apple cobbler and drams of a ten-year-old brandy, a wedding anniversary gift from Berry.

"We haven't had much reason to celebrate since Mary Margaret got married," Rebecca said somberly. "You know we've had hard times, with the floods and droughts. God is testing us. Thanks to Him and Berry, however, we are better off than some folks in the valley. We've got our health and we are together."

She lifted the glass to her thin lips and the brandy immediately gave color to her pallid cheeks. Brag never loved her more than at that moment.

The mail wasn't due until for another day and time crawled for Brag. He spent the day preparing the fields for planting and the night packing for a trip west, he hoped.

Berry arrived the next morning, the geldings covered with mud brought on by an all-night rain. He had new clothes, a box full of books and a new telegraph key Brag could use for practice.

The fact Berry brought the items hinted that he did indeed have the job. The cut of clothes spelled cold country. Brag suspected Berry probably already knew he had the job and even that it was out west.

Rebecca and the girls bustled about happily, packing Brag's new clothes in the Saratoga trunk Berry had brought.

"You should dig into those new books as soon as possible, Brag," Berry suggested. He blew away the vapors from a steaming cup of coffee as the rain cavorted on the tin roof. He and Sam discussed the harvest they had just reaped, fortunately before the rains descended over the valley.

"You are lucky," Berry said. "I stopped by Old Jake's place and his family is still in the fields. I'm not sure what the others did. I'll find out tomorrow."

Berry settled into a chair near the roaring fire and propped his feet on a rickety stool. He watched the children huddle on the floor near him, scribbling on the paper he provided. These quiet hours spent with the Coopers were warm and blissful, far from the turmoil of his businesses in Cincinnati.

Berry had often told Brag about his friendship with Sam and the Cooper family. He had known Sam more than twenty-five years, back when he was hacking out an existence on a small, rocky piece of land above the river. Five children had already swollen the Cooper clan by then, none of them able to provide the strong hands Sam needed to work the unyielding ground.

Sam's grit and fortitude in the face of the odds impressed Berry. He felt deep sympathy for Rebecca, not a physically strong woman and with such a wild brood to rear. He vowed to settle the family on more forgiving land, to snatch them from the shadow of near starvation. He bought the valley bottom land and moved the Coopers and their meager possessions to a plot close to Feesburg. He provided the tools and seeds, the Percheron and other necessities to get them started.

It was neither pity nor generosity that prompted Berry's actions. He had a stake in the land, too, and it must produce to pay a return.

He never regretted the move. Sam was a diligent, sober worker and Rebecca, despite her failing health, remained a constant, dedicated wife and mother. The Coopers quickly became Berry's favorite sharecroppers. He shared their happiness whenever another wrinkled, pink baby arrived at the farm with almost clockwork, two-year regularity.

The first was Mary Margaret, born on New Year's Day, 1861. She married Berry when she was twenty. Rebecca missed her help greatly after she moved into Berry's Cincinnati home.

Louetta came next in 1862, followed by Brag, Abner, Cora, William, Charles, Johnny and Alfred.

Brag knew Berry's caring and generosity also manifested itself with the Underground Railroad during the Civil War. He was one of many sympathetic supporters of anti-slavery in Cincinnati, hub of the semi-secret railroad.

Abolitionists doctrines were very unpopular in Brown County and those who held them were subject to much abuse. Among the strong anti-slavery leaders were Rev. Robert B. Dobbins and Dr. Isaac M. Beck of Sardinia, staunch friends of Berry.

Berry often harbored many an escaped Negro slave family on one of his farms hidden against the bluffs. It was an accomplishment that gave him much satisfaction and strengthened his faith in the Republicans. His clever hiding places and insistence on secrecy prevented political or financial pitfalls for Berry.

Now, Brag, his favorite among the Cooper children, was to escape the bleak destiny of pick and plow for another kind of railroad marching westward on shining steel rails.

Headed West

Brag waited eagerly on the road the next morning where the mail wagon would arrive with the letter.

He tore it open and quickly read the short paragraphs. His assignment was to Crawford, Nebraska, as an apprentice telegrapher on the Grand Island & Northern Wyoming Railroad. He was to report there as soon as possible. That was a puzzler. What had that railroad to do with the CB&Q Railroad? He'd have to ask Farswell, but his dream had come true.

There was bittersweet parting the next morning when Brag said good-bye to the family. When he kissed Rebecca, he had the terrible feeling he'd never see her alive again. And, as he turned to wave, he wondered if he'd ever see any of them again.

Farswell met them at the depot.

"I'm assigned to the Grand Island & Northern Wyoming

Railroad Company, Mr. Farswell, not the Q. How come?" Brag inquired.

"The Grand Island is an subsidiary of the Q which will build the line in Wyoming. You will actually be working for the Burlington. Just make the most of your experiences out there and good luck."

Berry gave Brag a strong hug and said, "As much as I love you, Sam, Rebecca and your brothers and sisters, I'm delighted to see you away from there.

"A whole, bright new world is out there just waiting for you to grab," Berry went on. "Just don't forget us folks back here, especially your family. Write often or, better still, send a telegram." He squeezed a roll of bills into Brag's hand.

The CG&PRR passenger express leaving Sardinia that afternoon would make connections in Cincinnati with the Pennsylvania Railroad's "Spirit of Chicago" to that burgeoning Queen City of the Midwest. There, Brag would catch the CB&Q's passenger local west through Omaha, then northwest to the tiny town of Crawford, Nebraska. It was a journey of nearly 1,000 miles.

The dizzying reality of being on his own did not hit Brag until he boarded the train.

He tingled with excitement as he settled into a seat in the crowded passenger car and pulled a book from the suitcase. It was a dog-eared copy of "The Chicago, Burlington & Quincy Railroad, Past, Present and Future," a history of the thirty-four-year-old line.

The railroad started as the Aurora Branch Railroad in 1849 with twelve miles of track in Illinois. By 1855, it had adopted the Chicago, Burlington & Quincy name, which best described its tracks stretching to Burlington, Iowa, and Quincy, Illinois, on opposite sides of the Mississippi River.

The Q completed its own line from Aurora to Chicago in 1864, with the distinction of running the first train into Chicago's newly opened Union Stockyards. Boston financier John Murray Forbes, Charles E. Perkins, now president, and now assistant administrator George W. Holdrege started the rapid rise of the Burlington, as it was known following the Civil War.

The road tripled in size because Forbes had undertaken a shrewd, careful amalgamation of more than two hundred smaller roads. Chief among Forbes' acquisitions were the Hannibal and St. Joseph Railroad and the Burlington & Missouri River Railroad. The former was heavily promoted by John M. Clemens, father of Samuel Clemens, better known as Mark Twain.

The H&St.J brought mail from the East across Missouri to connect with the Pony Express and developed the first rail car equipped to sort mail en route. The road also sparked the beginning of Kansas City as a rail center and gateway to the expanding southwest. Its workers also built the first railroad bridge across the Missouri River in 1869.

Meanwhile, the B&MR was building across Iowa, reaching the Missouri River in 1869 with heavy financial help from Forbes and his group of eastern backers. This was possible mainly because the road provided a natural westward extension of the growing Q. In 1868, the Burlington completed bridges across the Mississippi at Burlington and Quincy, linking the three lines.

However, in 1871, Jay Gould and his New York allies seized control of the Missouri line, using it as a pawn in bitter rate wars against the Burlington. By 1883, however, Perkins had re-purchased the line through a series of crafty political and financial maneuvers and it became an integral part of the Burlington system.

Plans to move westward into Nebraska were made during these years of difficult track-laying and adroit financial juggling. A separate company, the Burlington & Missouri Railroad in Nebraska, was formed and, in 1870, the line reached Lincoln, newly designated state capital and the Q headquarters.

A junction with the Union Pacific was reached at Kearney in 1872. By the time the Missouri River bridge was opened at Plattsmouth in 1880, the Nebraska branch had filled its territory with branch lines and moved into western Nebraska, its value to the Q now well established.

In 1880, the Q purchased the line outright and two years later, the road was completed into Denver, providing the Queen City of the West with its first direct mail route to Chicago over a single line.

The railroads were growing so fast that in the 1880 decade, more than 70,000 miles of track were laid.

Holdrege, a Harvard grad who started as a one-dollar-a-day timekeeper for the railroad, had outsmarted his chief rival, the Union Pacific Railroad. The UP considered all territory lying north of the Platte River as its private domain, firmly against any Burlington forces building across its sacrosanct land. Holdrege forced a bill through the 1886 Nebraska Legislature saying that if four-hundred feet of track were laid, it could not be torn up, but must be recognized as part of the railroad's expansion.

With that law, Holdrege slowed UP's track laying to a crawl. The practice was to grade many miles of roadbed in advance of the track-laying crew. Holdrege would allow the grading to continue for many miles. Then, in the dead of night, Holdrege's crews would quietly lay four-hundred feet of track across the UP roadbed, forcing the UP to re-grade in a different location. By such wily maneuvers, Holdrege held off the mighty Union Pacific and enabled the Burlington to advance northwest.

The grading crews earned twelve and a half cents per hour, about one dollar a day. A grading crewman who furnished his own horses or mules received an extra $1 per day, plus hay for his stock.

Brag would journey over these new rails to Crawford, where he would be assistant to one Terrance Day, a pioneer telegrapher with the Q.

As he read, Brag realized his good fortune stretched farther than he imagined. The Q wasn't going bankrupt like so many railroads had done and were doing even this day. If he passed the probationary period, his job was assured for many years to come.

The train picked its way along the Ohio River bluffs and the late afternoon sun threw golden squares on the coach floor as Brag continued to read.

The Northern Pacific was building west to Washington's Puget Sound. Railroad baron James Hill had connected his St. Paul, Minneapolis and Manitoba, later the Great Northern, with the Canadian Pacific, completing the first northern transcontinental railroad. It was obvious then that extension northwest would put Burlington into a position to move grain and lumber south while transporting coal and manufactured products north to the Pacific coast.

Brag was especially interested in the one chapter of the history.

As it expanded west, the Burlington become known as the "Granger Road" because of its close association with ranchers and farmers. Brag often heard his father and Berry discuss the Grange, which had reached its membership peak in 1875. The Grange's political and social ramifications little affected their farm life and Berry ignored it because it lacked political clout.

The Q, however, was deeply involved, not so much with the Grange as with the products of the farmers and ranchers. Its life blood was the shipment of these products to markets in the East and South.

Burlington representatives worked closely with farmers, advising them and prospective settlers on what crops could be successfully raised on the land-grant properties it sold to them. Alfalfa was introduced by Burlington people as a commercial crop in Nebraska in 1875. Crop, stock, irrigation and soil improvement and conservation were aggressively promoted by the Q.

Seed and soil exhibits and special poultry and stock trains were used by Burlington to bring the most advanced sciences then known directly to the farmers. The railroad even went so far as to employ farmers and ranchers in their shops during the winter months.

Congress extended land grants to Burlington in Missouri, Iowa and Nebraska, chiefly to promote expansion and settlement. To encourage settlement of the West, the U. S. Government granted the railroads twenty sections of land, or 12,800 acres, for each mile of track laid. Burlington had already been granted more than two-million acres in Nebraska alone.

Burlington even looked overseas to attract settlers, employing as many as two-hundred-fifty agents in the East and manned offices in England, Scotland, Sweden and Germany.

Such foresight was amply rewarded. From 1870 until 1887, Burlington sold more than two-million acres of land to more than twenty-thousand settlers.

Brag was impressed by Burlington's accomplishments and its long-time concern for the settler, farmer and cattleman. Had he known these facts earlier, he might have struck out long ago for the railroad life.

He tucked the book away and peered out the window as the train entered the bustling river town of Cincinnati.

Brag was impressed by his first train ride, the comfort of the coach and the easy speed which ate up the miles from Sardinia to Cincinnati. The noisy clatter of wheels as they crossed rail joints and switches, the uneven sway of the car and the smell of burning coal seemed part of him from long ago. Berry was right, he belonged to the railroad.

He was unpleasantly surprised when he boarded the "Spirit of Chicago" and handed the conductor the railroad pass Farswell had given him. The conductor nodded and smiled at him.

Brag was not impressed by the Pennsylvania Road. He was traveling in coach as an unpaid railway employee, not in the plush library-buffet car up ahead. The coach had double wicker seats on each side near the windows with an aisle down the middle. Spittoons were placed strategically down the aisle, but were often missed, leaving a crude mess on the floor. Pull blinds covered the windows. A coal stove stood at the leading end of the car and kerosene lamps hung on wall brackets along the car. A drinking water can with a dipper stood near the stove. The toilet was an open-hole stool surrounded by a partition at the back end of the car. Smoking was allowed.

An observation car replaced the caboose for use by first-class passengers. Brag discovered that only two classes of tickets were sold, coach or chair, and first-class for Pullman sleeping or dining car passengers.

Looking out the window, Brag caught sight of a young girl escorted by what he took to be her mother and father. By their dress, he knew they were first-class passengers walking toward the coach up ahead.

The girl was beautiful. Dark brown hair framed her pale face with a tiny nose and fragile cheeks. She looked up and their eyes met. She surveyed him with a measure of self-confidence, almost contempt, that surprised him. She wore a bright, blue bonnet that accentuated her delicate features. He smiled and she smiled back, then disappeared. He knew he just had to meet her.

The train jerked to a start and moved out of the station. Brag walked to the end of the car, opened the door and stood on the platform, peering into the next car. He was astonished at its elegance and his heart leaped as he saw her seated with her parents.

The conductor opened the coach door and asked sharply, "What are you doing here, young man?"

"I was just looking," Brag replied.

"Well, you have to pay extra to ride in here." He wheeled on his heels and closed the door.

Brag retreated to his seat. He wanted very much to meet the pretty girl in the bright blue bonnet.

Suddenly, he remembered the wad of bills Berry had given him. He retrieved it from his pocket and unrolled it.

"Three-hundred dollars!" he exclaimed out loud. The eyes of the passenger seated next to him grew wide as Brag glanced at him. Then Brag stuffed the wad back into his pocket, grimaced at the man and got up again.

He went to the door, saw a Negro porter midway down the coach and beckoned to him.

"What would it cost for me to get into that car?" Brag asked when the porter opened the door.

"I doesn't know, sir. I'll get the conductor."

"Oh, it's you again," the conductor said.

"I don't want to start any trouble, but what would it cost for me to get into that car?"

The conductor asked for his ticket and Brag gave him the Q pass Farswell had given him.

"Oh, a new Burlington employee, huh?" The conductor's demeanor softened then.

"I have an open seat. It's first-class and it'll cost you five dollars and another one dollar if you want to eat in the dining car," he said.

Brag peeled off the bills and handed them to the surprised conductor.

"I want next to that pretty girl, too," he said.

"Right this way, sir," he said, handing Brag back his Q pass, along with a brightly embossed first-class ticket.

Brag was not the least bit embarrassed as the conductor ushered him to a seat across from the young girl. She was even prettier close up, he concluded. Her mother, too, was good looking and her father eyed Brag with interest.

"Pardon me, young man, but where did you come from?" the girl's father asked as Brag sat down.

"From Ohio, sir."

"No, I mean how did you get a seat in this car?"

"Oh, well, I bought a ticket, sir."

"But, were you late getting on?"

"No, sir, I came from coach."

The man stared at Brag from boots to hat, obviously sizing him up. He stroked his Vandyke beard and seemed clearly in control of the situation.

"What is your name, young man?" he asked sharply.

"Brag Cooper, sir, all the way from Feesburg, Ohio. And your's?" Brag replied, extending his hand.

"I'm Winfield Scott Townsend, this is my wife, Jennie, and my daughter, Aletha." He shook hands, smiled and the ice was broken.

"May I inquire, Mr. Cooper, what is the nature of your business?" he asked.

Brag explained and Townsend laughed.

"What a coincidence! We live in Crawford and the railroad has just come there. We're all so excited about it. I run the Nash Finch Company there."

The girl remained silent during their conversation, nodding and smiling whenever Brag spoke.

Their conversation was mainly about Brag's family, which he gladly told, and the Depression still gripping the country after the Civil War. It ended with the porter's bell call to dinner.

Brag joined the Townsends at the dining car table. Several times he caught Aletha staring at him. Each time, she smiled and looked away. He felt they had met somewhere before, but put that down to her faint resemblance to his sister, Mary Margaret.

Two hours later, the train pulled into Chicago's Union Station.

Brag and the Townsends made the long walk to the opposite end of the station where the Q train stood. Six coach cars, a Pullman and an observation car made up the train. It would be hauled west by a high-wheeled locomotive. An impressive sight, Brag concluded.

He boarded, noting the conservative interior with its polished wooden floor, colorful window drapes and brass corner lanterns. There was no dining car so they would buy meals at the railroad beaneries along the five-hundred-mile route to Omaha.

The passengers, he noticed, were of a rougher cut than his previous traveling companions. The Townsends occupied the seats opposite Brag, but he did so want to sit next to Aletha.

The man grunted heavily as Brag eased into the seat next to him. Brag peered at him out of the corner of his eye.

He was barrel-chested, covered head to toe in weathered buckskin. A gaudy, red shirt poked out at his throat and wrists, like blood spurting from an amputated limb. A hat, origin unknown to Brag, covered his face as he snored loudly. A buffalo hunter or maybe a genuine mountain man, Brag surmised.

"What's that you say, son?" a coarse voice suddenly asked. "Are you mumbling to me?"

"No, sir, I didn't say a word," Brag replied, smiling as the stranger poked his hat back and stared at him.

"I gives a man a wide berth who talks to hisself, son. But, I can see you ain't old enough yet to be loco," he chuckled.

The man smiled broadly, uniform teeth competing with the whiteness of his beard, and extended a rough, meaty hand.

"Name's Smith, son, Percival Smith, no relation whatever to Jedediah, fortunately. I guess yer headed for Colorado and the gold diggins, right?"

The stranger's directness caught Brag off guard.

"No, as a matter of fact, I'm headed to Nebraska to work for this railroad," he said timidly. "I'll bet you're on your way to Colorado, though."

Smith snorted, shook his head emphatically and said, "You'd lose that bet, son. By the way, never did catch your name?"

"Cooper, sir, Brag Sanford Cooper, come by way of Ohio," he replied, warming to the stranger.

"Well, don't that beat all. This new-fangled railroad's sure the thing fer toting a feller across the country. Why I'll bet we're doing a full forty miles per hour, don't you think, Mr. Cooper? I sure do like them sleepin' accommodations, too, almost like bedding down with a soft, warm Indian squaw."

"You've done that?" Brag gasped.

"Done it? Why, son, I practically invented the practice way back in '59 when I ran with Jim Bridger in the Yallerstone mountains."

He caught the interest in Brag's face and quickly went on. He also knew that the pretty, young lady across the way was a captive audience, too, and he made the most of it.

"I remember we were camped one day on the shores of Shoshone Lake when this band of peace-loving Souix showed up. Course, this was long before Custer got kilt at the Little Big Horn and before them cussed gold rushers stirred up the Black Hills.

"This was a trustin' bunch of redskins and they knew Jim

from away back."

He paused, pulled a plug of black tobacco from his pocket and bit off a chunk.

"Well, mister, we and a bunch of trappers had settled in fer the night after a mighty delirious day of huntin', hollerin' and hootin' just fer the fun of it. We called it, from then on, Rendezvous. Them Indians heard the commotion and came riding out of the hills to see what was going on.

"We got to signin' and tradin' with old Jim doing most of the signin' 'cause he was the only one understood their signs.

"Well, old Jim didn't cotton to fraternizing with them Indians 'cept businesswise. He was straight with them, never gave them no hootch or nothing. Me and the boys got it down to secret cases, though. Them braves would bring in a couple of squaws in exchange for a batch of the Red Eye we always mixed up."

He paused, stroked his beard and pondered for a moment.

"Ya know, I don't suppose that was any different from them city slickers I've seen in Denver and Cheyenne, plying them poor, white dancing girls full of hootch and nailing 'em in the cribs. We are a bit more civilized out there in the hills, though. Straight forward bargaining, no beatin' around the bush. We each had somethin' the other wanted.

"Mr. Cooper, one of them squaws turned out to be jest about the prettiest dern woman I've seen this side of St. Looie and I was right hard pressed to keep her to myself. I still think to this day that, after I had my way with her, she made the rounds of the camp. And, that's the truth of the matter, Mr. Cooper."

Brag believed the man's story because he wanted to. Here was the West in all its primitive glory, just like he'd read in the penny novels Berry often brought to the farm. He believed Smith was a honest-to-God mountain man, sitting right here beside him.

"That's one helluva yarn, Mr. Smith," he said. "But, us Ohio boys were brought up to believe all Indians are savages, murdering, scalping and raping innocent women and children, stealing and burning. That's all true, isn't it?"

Smith frowned and nailed the aisle spittoon with a stream of tobacco.

"Half of them stories is hogwash," he scowled. "Sure, they'd scalp and loot, but you gotta remember it was us white men what came in and stole their land, shot their buffalo, trapped their beaver and plowed under their sacred ground. And the French was the first folks to massacre and do the scalping, too."

He spit again and settled back to ponder his words.

"The Army tried to make peace, but it was the Army what massacreed the Cheyenne and Arapaho at Sand Creek and broke more treaties than the Indians ever did."

He was turning what started as a casual, friendly conversation into a soapbox sermon, Brag thought.

"I don't believe, like most folks, that the only good Indian is a dead Indian and General Sheridan who said that is an ass," he rambled on.

"Put yourself in their place, Mr. Cooper. Suppose some strangers came in and killed your family, stomped all over your property and stole your livestock? How would you react? We gotta learn to live with the Indians or these damned wars will go on forever."

Brag shook his head and dared disagree with him.

"I'm not old enough to have opinions, I guess, but I'd say both sides are right, in their own way, and too stubborn to give ground to the other," he said.

"You've got a bright head on your shoulders, young man," Smith laughed. "You'll make out all right, I suspect."

The hat fascinated Brag. "What's that you're wearing, a Stetson?"

"No, Mr. Cooper, it's a Hudson Bay Felt, made out of beaver pelts."

Brag had to have one, but was reluctant to ask Smith.

The train pulled into St. Joseph and they elbowed their way through the passengers to stretch their cramped legs on the boarding platform. A brisk westerly swirled up dust clouds in the street and they could feel the first chill of an oncoming winter.

Brag had not eaten since leaving Chicago and the fascination with Aletha and Smith's wild stories had until now kept the hunger pangs at bay.

After the train pulled out, he bought a couple of cold sandwiches and a cold drink from the news butcher hawking his goods through the train. He wanted to buy for Aletha, too, but Winfield beat him to the draw.

The car, loaded with fresh, new faces, headed north and crossed the Missouri River over Burlington's new bridge at Falls City. It would curl west and head into Nebraska with one hundred miles and three hours to go until Omaha.

Smith had pulled the hat over his nose and gone to sleep, so Brag cracked open the latest edition of Bullinger's Postal Guide and began to read. He leafed through the section on Nebraska, circling postal stops he thought might be important to his job.

The Railroader's Bible, the Book of Rules given him by Farswell, gave him insights on railroad terminology and so much of it was strange language to him.

The pay for a locomotive engineer, Brag learned, was sixty dollars per month, no extra for extra miles, and he was docked if he logged less than 2,500 miles a month. Switchman, the lowest on the railroad ladder, earned forty dollars per month. Promotions went switchman to yard brakeman, to freight brakeman to freight conductor or passenger brakeman to passenger conductor. A switchman's job was to line up and couple cars in the order that the cars would be set out along the line. A brakeman cranked down or released the hand brakes on the cars while running on the line. He also picked up and set out cars at stations along his run.

Telegraph operators carried a box relay they could hook up to the telegraph wires anywhere along the line to send and receive messages. Station agents were required to know Morse Code and send and receive messages. Other duties included repairing broken telegraph lines, keeping equipment in working order and managing the office.

Brag was familiar with several station agents in Sardinia,

but more familiar with the hobos, or bos, who frequently stopped by their farm for a hand-out. Berry had once told him about hobos. "A hobo works and wanders," he said, "a tramp dreams and wanders and a bum drinks and wanders."

There was railroad slang, like poke-out, for food; hoppins for vegetables; gumps for chicken and other slang Brag would have to know. There was also parlor car, sections, one or more trains running on the same schedule; varnish, a high-class passenger train; heavy iron; sourdoughs; Red Eye; Leadville Mule, a strong whiskey; Monongahela and Louis Roederer's, an 1865 vintage of the hard stuff.

He also learned the railroads had division points for coaling and watering, usually twenty or thirty miles apart, depending on the terrain. And, that the Q's passenger trains usually averaged about thirty-five miles an hour.

Brag was half way through the book when the conductor called out the Omaha stop, bringing Smith to life and stirring up the other passengers.

They stared out the window for their first glimpse of the former territorial capital, now a booming trade center for the railroads and river shipping on the Missouri and Platte rivers.

Here, as per instructions in the letter, Brag was to meet David Bowdein, territorial agent for the Q, who would brief him on his job, then send him on to Lincoln.

He said good-bye to Smith with a twinge of sadness, for he liked the old mountain man right from the start.

"May never see you again, Mr. Cooper," Smith said softly, gripping Brag's hand in a strong, double-fisted grasp. "Try to remember old Percival Smith now and again and take to heart some of the things we discussed."

Brag watched the old man walk through the depot and disappear into the crowd, buckskin fringes swinging to the rhythm of his jaunty walk. He felt part of the past, and the future, had just walked out of his life.

His future walked in when Bowdein sauntered up and introduced himself.

Crawford, Nebraska

Crawford, Nebraska, was a typical train town, sprouting suddenly in the middle of nowhere like the fields of sunflowers along the Burlington tracks.

Brag's arrival came on the heels of a bustling boom in Crawford. The town had been born only four years before with the arrival of the railroad as its tracks plodded steadily northwest. It reverberated to busy railroad crews, construction gangs, cowboys, ranchers, trappers, mountain men and the usual crop of con men. A platoon of Negro soldiers on liberty from nearby Fort Robinson added a festive holiday atmosphere as Brag stepped off the train.

In one sweep of his eye, Brag took in the town. It consisted of a car switching yard, a switch tower, water tanks, a coaling shed, depot and a roundhouse, pride of the town. There were the Red Cloud Agency and the Nash Finch wholesale grocer out of Minneapolis, Townsend's store. A collection of churches, saloons, hotels, eateries and resident houses dotted the once barren, rolling land. Dust was everywhere, churned up by the hooves and wheels of a working town and swirled along by cooling breezes from the Black Hills several miles to the north.

Crawford sat about forty miles east of Van Tassel and was surrounded almost equidistantly by Harrison, Chadron, Adelia and Belmont. Belmont, thirteen miles southeast, was the site of the famous Belmont Tunnel, gouged out that same year in the Pine Ridge area, a high promontory overlooking the surrounding countryside. The tunnel was constructed for a connection with the proposed Fremont, Elkhorn & Missouri Valley Railroad, which would run west to Douglas and Casper, Wyoming, and north into the Black Hills. Crawford Hill rose eight-hundred feet, forcing the railroad to double-head trains with two locos or use the more powerful mallet locos to get over it.

Townsend shook Brag's hand and said he could be reached at his store. However, he could only wave at Aletha and watch them move off in their carriage in a cloud of dust.

The railroad depot stood in the middle of the town, a modest, wooden structure atypical of the false-front buildings thrown up at end-of-track in Burlington's headlong rush to Montana.

A formidable looking man sporting a large, handlebar moustache approached Brag and asked, "Mr. Cooper, I presume?"

"Yes, sir," Brag responded, looking directly into the man's piercing blue eyes. He stood solidly, his brawny, towering body blocking most of the sun.

"My name's Terrance Day. I'm the station agent here. Come on and we'll get you started."

The railroad office was a clean, neat room crammed with acid batteries, insulators, telegraph keys, books, papers and cabinets, one jammed with rifles and pistols. Day piled a stack of papers in front of Brag and told him to fill them out, all the while asking numerous questions about his life. When he seemed satisfied, Day pointed him toward the hotel, loaded him with timetables, maps and the Consolidated Book of Railroad Rules for the Q and said, "Get a room, memorize these and be here tomorrow morning at six."

Fifteen bucks to the hotel clerk got Brag two months' board and a tiny, clean room overlooking the town. He stared out at the sun setting in a brown haze and wondered if Day would be as tough to work for as he looked.

Whatever, he was now firmly embarked on his railroad career and looked forward eagerly to his first day.

A ruckus in town that night failed to awaken Brag and he wasn't aware of it until he reported the next morning.

"Killed a soldier last night, they did," Day said abruptly as he sat with Brag at the telegrapher's desk.

A Negro soldier from Fort Robinson's Ninth U. S. Cavalry had lost heavily in a card game, Day explained. He and his buddies retreated to the fort for reinforcements and, when they came back into town, a battle royal ensued. The soldiers rode down the main street, shooting and shouting and the townspeople responded in kind.

"When it was all over, a soldier was dead in the street," Day said. "The Army will hold an investigation, of course, but I doubt anything will come of it. People I talk to say they never heard a shot."

"I sure didn't hear a thing," Brag responded.

"Well, I hope your ears are better with that relay or you're in trouble.

"I want you to be completely familiar with what's going on with our general contractors, the KB&C, the B&M and the GI&NWRC in general," Day explained. Brag was thoroughly confused by this alphabet soup Day had suddenly served him.

"Here, in a nutshell, is where we're at," Day went on, unfolding a large, topographic map across the table.

"There are three, soon to be four, companies involved here," Day explained, tracing the routes with his finger. "The

Burlington & Missouri River Railroad crews are working in Nebraska and South Dakota. The Kilpatrick Brothers and Collins, our construction people, are already carving track bed across this line into northeastern Wyoming.

"The Grand Island & Northern Wyoming Railroad is building the road from Dakoming, in Wyoming Territory, to Sheridan and on into Montana. We, the Q, are negotiating to lease all the GI&NWR property and right-of-way and most probably will do so very soon.

"Last month our crews cut the grade over the old Cheyenne-Deadwood stage road to Newcastle, Wyoming. The rails should be complete there by early next month. Edward Gillette, once with the Denver & Rio Grande Railroad, is now our chief surveyor.

"Last year, an old prospector named Mikkel Gladhough found coal in Fuller Canyon on the Little Oil Creek, seven miles north of Newcastle. What is now the Cambria field is huge, right near the surface and Burlington has laid claim to it. Cambria town sprung up almost overnight and they've already built a spur line down to where our road will come into Newcastle, sometime in December, we hope."

Brag had his nose to the map and one ear tuned to the relay. He didn't want to miss a thing.

Day went on.

"Now, from Newcastle, another party has surveyed the route out about thirty miles. Gillette and his gang will start over from Newcastle because that other party did a poor job. We've got to get to a cattle loading point by next summer or the Q will lose a big contract with the cattlemen up in northern Wyoming.

"Gillette is now surveying the new route and setting up probable coaling stops every thirty to forty miles and watering stops every twenty miles or so. I don't know what the new towns west of Newcastle will be named, but I suspect after men of our survey and contracting parties, local folks or B&M people."

Suddenly, the telegraph key began clicking. Day didn't

need to jot down the message, automatically assembling the dots and dashes in his head.

"It's from Gillette near Newcastle. Says his telegrapher got snake-bit last night. Wants us to send him another, so you'll go."

"But, I just got here. I don't know the country and I don't know my keying all that well," Brag protested, his heart pounding.

"Don't argue, son," Day responded sharply. "You'll go and you'll do the job. No better way for you to catch on than to stomp around out there in the boondocks with Gillette, where things are really happening. I wish I could go myself."

Day may have been gruff in ordering Brag to his first big job, but Brag liked the idea and began to like the man, too.

"You get over to the hotel, pack your trail duds and I'll send Jimmy over with the buckboard. If you need anything, get it at Nash Finch and charge the Q. We'll grub you and you'll sleep in a tent."

Brag had little time to ponder his new orders because Jimmy was in front of the hotel before he'd thrown his heavy clothes into a suitcase.

"Come on, Mr. Cooper, we've got to git to Newcastle afore dark," Jimmy shouted. "We can miss the trail and the horse he don't like the night." Jimmy was Negro and Brag sensed in his demeanor that he didn't cotton to the night, either.

Newcastle lay about one-hundred miles northwest across the rolling prairie. As they bounced along in the hard-riding buckboard, Jimmy explained why he feared the journey.

The wagon trail led across a corner of the new state of South Dakota, several dangerous river fords and through Sioux Indian territory. That was the big stopper for Jimmy. The Sioux had a year to live as a great tribe before the battle at Wounded Knee. That last great Indian battle would send them to a reservation. Small Sioux raiding parties were still active in the area.

Brag could see the uneasiness in Jimmy's quick whip on

the horse. "Gotta git there 'afore dark and the Sioux," he exclaimed.

As they rattled along, Brag took in the scenery. It was nothing like home. Long, rolling, grass covered hills were broken only occasionally by an arroyo or dry creek bed and cottonwoods and scrub brush sprouted infrequently along a rare trickle of water. The wagon trail had been cut first, followed by the road bed. Brag noted the good workmanship and the fact the rails hadn't been laid. They waved to a couple of road gangs on the way.

"Sure a lot of space out here, Jimmy," he cracked.

"Sure, but I dasn't need it all."

"What do you mean?"

"Well, I'd come out here last year from M'sippi where things is bright and green and pretty," he said, the taut muscles in his bare brown arms reacting to the pull of the reins.

"There ain't a thing out here 'cept rattlesnakes, dust and Indians."

"You afraid of the Indians?" Brag asked, watching his eyes for a reaction.

"Yas, sir, Mr. Cooper, sure is 'fraid of 'em and the snakes, too. They say there's renegades still out in them hills who'd jest as soon skin us both alive, white or black."

Brag got a reaction, all right, but it was his.

"You mean that seriously, Jimmy?" his eyes anxiously scanning the far hills.

"Bet yer scalp, I do!"

Jimmy's eyes widened and his knuckles turned white as he tightened his grip on the reins. They didn't talk now and Brag could picture wild, screaming Sioux suddenly plunging down around them.

The horse seemed unabashed by their apprehension and the buckboard bounced merrily along, raising a small cloud of dust which Brag was sure was a smoke signal to any lurking Sioux. He shook it off, but tucked the Remington rifle between his legs, just in case.

They'd come about forty miles now, crossing the South

Dakota border and fording several small creeks which re-
freshed the tired, dusty horse.

"We'll stop ta rest a few hours at Edgemont," Jimmy said
as the town came into view over a hill. "Can't stay long,
though, gotta keep moving."

Edgemont was another of those thrown-up railroad towns.
It lay in the shallow Cheyenne River valley some seven miles
north of a larger railroad stop, Provo. Both towns were about
eighty miles south of the notorious gold camp of Deadwood
City. The Deadwood Cheyenne stage route lay to the west and
the grading crews were pretty much following it for the
roadbed.

Jimmy changed horses at the corral and they ate at the
railroad beanery. Brag struck up a conversation with the
Edgemont operator, Chuck Wilson, who was aware of the
situation.

"I suppose you're wondering why Gillette didn't ask for
me," Wilson said. "Well, I got the message, of course, but Day
told me several days ago that if anything like this came up, he
preferred to send out the new man—and you're it."

Brag laughed, but was flattered by the thought that Day
had him in mind all along.

They were on their way again, headed more north than
west into Wyoming Territory. The fresh horse eagerly followed the trail along the roadbed which led through depot
stops at Marietta, Argentine, Dewey, Dakoming and Clifton
and into Newcastle.

The sun was just touching the top of Elk Mountain south
of Newcastle when Jimmy reined in at Newcastle, greeted by
a smiling Ed Gillette.

"Made good time, huh, Jimmy?" he said, eyeing Brag
curiously.

"You're the new telegraph operator, right?" he asked,
unloading Brag's kit and vigorously shaking his hand.

"Yes sir, my first job."

"Well, we'll break you in proper out here, that's for sure."
He led Brag to a group of seven large canvas tents and

introduced him to his survey party, a rough, sturdy lot, Brag observed.

"Well, this is Newcastle, in all its glory," Gillette bellowed with a laugh, making a grand sweep with his arm.

Gillette was a broad-shouldered, bald-headed man with a bushy moustache and piercing eyes. Yet, he was an amiable man, Brag thought.

"Your tent is over here. You'll share it with five other men. The telegraph tent is just over there so you won't miss a thing.

"Right now, best you wire Day that you've arrived safe and are ready to go," Gillette continued. "We'll be up about dawn, so you'd better chow down now and turn in. You can meet up with our folks later tomorrow."

The heavy canvas tent had a fly hung out front as an awning. It was staked solidly to the ground and surrounded by a ditch to drain away the sudden, cold autumnal rains. Dirt was piled around the tent base to keep out the drafts and a board divided the tent in half, one for sleeping quarters for the men. The floor was covered with straw and then a wagon sheet, tarpaulins and blankets. A coal oil lantern hung on the center pole of the tent, casting dancing shadows across the wind-blown canvas. A small, sheet-iron stove glowing orange threw out minimal heat in the vastness of the tent. There were plenty of blankets and Brag was looking forward to spending his first night on the prairie in relative comfort.

He practiced his message to Day a couple of times before opening the telegraph key, then sent his very first railroad message nearly one-hundred miles back down the line. He was amazed and delighted when Day's reply came back, quick and crisp through the relay. Day's message also included a good-luck and Brag was proud that he copied it down so quickly and easily. Things were looking up, he thought, as he tucked the rough wool blanket tight against his head and fell asleep.

Six burly, laughing men, one banging a kettle, brought Brag abruptly awake the next morning.

"Morning, Mr. Cooper, welcome to Wyoming Territory,"

they chorused in unison. "We'd be honored to have the pleasure of your company at breakfast, if you please, sir." It was the beginning of a warm respect and great humor Brag received from the other hands.

Brag leaped from his bunk and the dry, cold air immediately penetrated his long johns. He splashed cold water in his face, dressed and joined the crew in the mess tent. The sun was not yet awake.

His first range breakfast was hearty, heavy and hot. A slab of bacon sizzled merrily on the griddle, an army of fried eggs marched beside sourdough hotcakes and the sharp aroma of black coffee filled the air.

"Help yourself, son," Gillette said, "stoke up good, it'll be a long, hard day."

So far, Gillette had not outlined Brag's duties, but that soon came.

"You wire Day that the other telegrapher is doing just fine over in Edgemont and that we'll be surveying up past Oil Creek today. We'll also need more staples by the end of the week. They will come up to end of track on the work train. Also, Jimmy will give our first surveys to the train crew. Then wire him you're going out with me on the survey. Can you remember all that? Here, I'll write it down for you."

"Not necessary, sir," Brag exclaimed. "Got it all in my head."

"Good man, Coop, you'll do just fine."

Brag wired the message and got a surprising one in reply. Elly, he called Aletha that in his mind now, had stopped at the office to ask about him. Brag's heart pounded a little faster.

"Pack your key and other equipment on the mule and take your warm duds," Gillette instructed. "Got any rain gear? Well, better draw some from Mike over there, he's our quartermaster. Our tents are warmer than some hotels I've slept in, but it rains a lot out here this time of year. We might even get some snow before we're through."

The party would string the telegraph wire for Brag over sagebrush, trees, anything to get it off the ground, as they moved ahead. The solid, iron wire connected in at Newcastle. Gillette left nothing to chance and the telegraph and Brag were their only link to civilization.

The survey party consisted of a transitman, head chainman, rear chainman, back flagman, stake marker and driver, levelman, rodman, topographer and his assistant; three teamsters, a hunter and a cook. Their pack train of twenty mean, sturdy mules was essential in the rough country as were their own mounts, the mule skinner and the camp dog. No survey party worth its salt went without a dog. Their's was a black and white cur named Judy, who greeted Brag with a snarl.

"Don't worry, kid, Judy likes only the men she knows in the party," said Jake, the cook. "She'll get used to you after she gets your smell down."

Jake went on to explain why Judy was so important. Camp dogs were used to warn of marauding Indians, other prowlers and wildlife. Army fort commanders on the frontier hired Indian scouts to whip and abuse their dogs until the dogs hated the sight and smell of an Indian. No trapper, mountain man or survey party ventured into the unknown without a faithful camp dog. Most were of mixed breed, usually a hunting hound and wolf crossed.

The party's hunter and scout was a towering, broad-shouldered Canadian named Pierre, who provided meat and fowl for the party. It was part of the contract the Q had with W. F. Cody, otherwise known as Buffalo Bill Cody, who provided meat to the grading crews and survey parties.

Brag was more interested in the mules than anything in the camp. He walked over to the tether and watched Jerry Grosthwaite tend to the twenty mules. He was touched by how gentle Grosthwaite was with the burly animals. He thought how much easier life on the Feesburg farm could have been with a pair of the powerful animals.

"You seem to have a touch with them, Jerry," he called.

"Got to know them, got to love them, too," Grosthwaite responded as he checked the foreleg of one of his charges. "They are probably the smartest four-legged animal in the world." He walked over, leaned against a tree next to Brag and rolled the makings. "Want a smoke, kid?" he asked. Brag shook his head, his eyes still on the mules.

"Yes, I like mules," Grosthwaite said, "been around them all my life. A mule ranks right up there with all the best brains in the animal world, and he's dependable, too. A mule won't drink to a bloat, won't cross an unsafe bridge and won't overeat, even in a field of green corn. A mule knows when the sun's too hot, the day is too cold and when he's done his day's work. Try to get a mule to work after he thinks he's done his share. Why, it's like trying to pull teeth from a dinosaur."

Brag laughed and asked for the makings. He had smoked a cigar or two back at the farm and preferred them. Here, in good company, a butt seemed to fit the mood.

"You watch as we work them in the field," Jerry went on. "You'll see they have a great sense of humor. They can be as comical as a clown and as somber as a judge. Yes, I love 'em, couldn't do without them."

Gillette walked up then, looked at the sky and put his arm around Brag's shoulder.

"You're going to get real familiar with the earth out here, son," he said with a broad smile.

"I'm already familiar with it, I'm a dirt farmer from back east, remember?" Brag replied. Gillette laughed.

The survey party wound its way out of Newcastle, breaking new ground with every step as it headed northwest toward the Big Horn Range, misty in the distance. Gillette said they were at least one-hundred-fifty miles away, but the cold, dry air made it seem closer.

The men rode easy in their saddles, but Brag was not a horseman. The only riding he had done was on the farm's old Percheron, and that was without a saddle for only short distances. By noon time, Brag's butt and legs were burning with the unaccustomed exertion and the pain was creeping up his back and shoulders.

They skirted the western foot of the Black Hills, which lost their height as they spread south and east onto the Great Plains.

The Black Hills were an isolated upheaval of rock in the midst of the so-called Great American Desert. They were some fifty miles wide and one hundred miles long, north to south. Travelers on their Western migrations said they "could see forever" across the plains, until they saw the Black Hills.

Gillette and his crew would top a hill, scan the surrounding territory through binoculars and make notes and drawings. Even though the Cambria find provided the Q with abundant coal for its locomotives, Gillette explained, it was best to survey and lay out the line along the easiest route. "Save a lot of manpower hours, coal and money that way," he said.

By the end of the day, they had surveyed and mapped about ten miles of territory, and Brag could barely walk.

"It sure felt like we covered more than ten miles," Brag said as he gingerly dismounted. He rubbed his butt, did a few deep-knee bends and moaned.

Gillette laughed. "Not been on a horse recently, huh, Brag? Well, get Jake to pour some liniment on you. Make you burn for a while, but it'll take the ache out. Be careful of your vitals, though.

"Always seems like more miles because we double back, recheck and stop more often than a mountain man might in making tracks," Gillette explained. "We've got to note every gully, draw, creek, tree, whatever and that takes time and a lot of scurrying around. Still in all, I suppose it's the only way. We can't fly like the hawks you saw today.

"Take some comfort that all you have is a sore ass," Gillette laughed. "How would you like to be on the road gang? They have to lay at least five miles of track a day behind us if we're going to come in under contract."

The hills around them were loaded with game—deer, elk, antelope, squirrels, ducks and geese, grouse and the coyote, the Tenor of the Prairie. Pierre was soon back with a dozen sage grouse and a young antelope. Jake turned some of the game into their evening meal, the rest he salted down or smoked for another day.

As they sat around the wind-blown camp fire, talking and

smoking, Brag felt more at peace with himself and the world than he ever had before.

It was like a new world out here, Brag thought. The sky was high, clean and crisp and the horizon stretched unspoiled in all directions.

The men were warm and friendly. They were a rough lot, he admitted as he watched their faces flicker golden in the firelight. They were of kin, friendly yet independent, purposeful without being dogmatic and totally without prejudice.

This was a new consciousness Brag had never felt on the farm. It was a kind of fraternity he never knew before, here under the sparkling western stars.

The Lone Rider

One day around Christmas, 1889, when the crew was about forty miles northwest of Cambria, a lone rider rode up.

Out here in virgin country Jake said it was unusual to see someone alone this far out in the boondocks.

The man rode tall and thin in the saddle astride a beautiful pinto horse, his Stetson pulled down so hard that Brag could barely see his face. His eyes were dark slits, a black moustache covered his mouth and black, silver-tipped hair poked out around his Stetson. He carried a Winchester rifle on his saddle and a Colt .45 on his hip.

The party gathered around the rider and Gillette extended a friendly hand, which the rider accepted with some hesitation.

"Welcome, stranger," Gillette said. "Cup of coffee, breakfast, maybe?"

The rider climbed easily from the horse, said his name was Justin Dvorak and that he had a small spread several miles to the northwest. He cradled the cup of coffee in his hands, blew the steam away and studied Gillette through narrow slits.

"You surveying a railroad through here?" he asked, finally.

Gillette nodded, swung his arm toward the northwest and said, "Yep, all the way to Billings. We'll join up with the Northern Pacific there."

"Well, if that don't beat all," Dvorak said. "I left a farm in Kansas two years ago because the railroad cut my land in two. Figured I'd move further out west and get away from it. But, here you are.

"Say, you didn't deliberately follow me all the way from Kansas, did you?" Dvorak inquired with a straight face.

Gillette and the party doubled over with laughter and Dvorak, momentarily puzzled by it all, had to laugh, too.

Gillette assured him that, yes, the railroad had indeed dogged his tracks all the way from Kansas.

"Why, we've had spies following you all the way from Kansas, just to mark where you might settle down. When you finally did, they reported back to the railroad and they sent us out to run our railroad right to your front door.

"Seems you have a natural instinct for picking out the most likely route for the railroad and we're just making do with a good thing."

Gillette slapped Dvorak on the back, roared with laughter and offered him another cup of coffee.

"No thanks," Dvorak said with disgust. "I might have guessed that was it when I spied your gang several days ago. Guess I'll be moving on."

He climbed into the saddle, jerked the reins tight and fired one parting shot.

"If you're thinking of following me west, then you'd better get plenty of men and blasting powder. I'm headed for the Tetons!"

With that, he rode off into the sunset.

The party woke every morning now with Oil Creek and the last range of the Black Hills and Mount Pisgah distant to the east.

The Black Hills stopped abruptly at Newcastle and Oil Creek. The land now shaped out as a series of low, rolling hills, scarred by numerous dry gulches with occasional rivulets of alkali water. These arroyos could fill quickly with the sudden thunderstorms common year around and become raging, white-water death traps for man and beast. Buffalo grass, about knee-high and stretching as far as the eye could see, waved gently in the breeze. Gillette said its high nutritional content, especially in protein, was why the bison flourished and why cattlemen so prized the Great Prairie.

Gillette's survey methods were tried and true. The party ran careful preliminary lines over every possible route the road could take, then by comparison, selected the best. As a rule, the best route would be the easiest grade, with consideration given to the cost of the construction. When survey instruments determined the most favorable route, a preliminary location would be made. This would be improved by fitting the route into the topography of the country. Shallow cuts were avoided because of snow drifts and the sunny side of a valley was always preferred. Gillette said he often pictured the route in his sleep as simply as possible. Bridges, overpasses and tunnels were to be avoided if possible because of their high costs in dollars and manpower. Often the route followed centuries-old buffalo trails, the animals by instinct picking out the easiest ground.

The survey party's maps, drawings and charts then went back to Omaha where the final route was determined, usually by Ivan Weeks, Burlington's chief engineer.

The camp routine after a cold, hard day of riding, would find Gillette holding court in the headquarters tent. He would review the day's work, get the topographer, James, and the draftsman, Richard, to refine their maps, and discuss the next day's work.

"I have a philosophy about this railroad," he exclaimed that night as they gathered around the fire. "Most of you have worked for me for a long time, but I want to refresh your minds how I feel about the Burlington and the way we work the routes.

"Our idea is to get not only the best route for the company, but to secure the cheapest route for moving the products of the country as a benefit to the public, regardless of who might run the railroad," he began.

"We keep a clean camp, provide the best mounts and food and hire the best cook, like Jake here. Our regard for those factors and a human regard for the welfare and comfort of you men enables us to hire only the very best for our survey parties and to keep them. We don't pay as much compared to other railroads, but I feel the men we hire are the best in the business.

"All of this has a direct bearing on the results we obtain out on the job as the road gangs grade through the line. I believe in this mightily and I want all of you to know that."

Gillette dismissed the men, but called Brag to the mapping table.

"I want you to always be aware of where we are, what we're doing and what we're about to do," he said.

"You'll wire Day every night, like you've been doing, with our progress. Here's a list of topo readings and the things we've done so far, so get that off tonight."

Keying his nightly messages back to Day had became so routine to Brag that often his mind wandered back to Elly and their meeting on the train. He didn't think of her much, except when he sparked up his key and knew his words were being received in the town where she lived.

Day came back that night with another note from Elly. "She says hello and hopes to see you again soon," the relay spelled out in the sharp, even clicks that were the mark of Day's experienced hand. That was all.

Brag fired back, "Me, too."

It was best, he thought, not to burden Day with his personal thoughts, knowing Day's strict adherence to the railroad telegrapher's code. Still, he wondered what she was doing, how she was getting along.

He could still picture her pretty face as crisply in his mind as the key clicks. He really didn't long for her in that sense, since Gillette kept him so busy during the day and the evenings were occupied with sending and recording messages.

Brag had never been in love and doubted he was now. Yet, in fleeting moments her image haunted him. When it did, he felt a spark through his body, like when he accidently touched the telegraph battery leads.

It wasn't the Sioux which rode out of the hills to greet the survey party the next morning. It was a band of angry cowboys.

Yelling and shouting, they surrounded Brag and the party, pistols holstered, but rifles waving in the air.

Gillette stood his ground, pistol also holstered, but hands raised in a sign of peace, as if they really were Sioux.

"What do you want?" he asked sharply. From his coolness, Brag surmised Gillette had been through this before.

"We want you and your gang off our land," shouted the hardest looking rider of the bunch. "You got legal papers saying you can bust through here?"

The man rode straight in the saddle, his grimy Stetson pulled to one side so that the sun had comically tanned one side of his face, not the other. There was no smile underneath the Stetson.

"Where you from?" Gillette asked.

"The Circle T Ranch, if it's any of your damn business, mister," he shouted.

"Well, seems to me the railroad's already bought this land from one Mr. Thomas K. Terrell and he has the papers, if my memory serves me correctly, mister," Gillette responded. "If you knew your business like you all seem to know how to shout and holler, you'd know that."

"Don't seem as I recollect that name, mister," the man shouted, louder than Gillette or the party needed to hear. It was obvious that the man knew he was riding on uneven ground because he kept shouting louder.

"You and that gang of yours out just to raise some hell?" Gillette asked. "Seems to me the place for that is back on your ranch or over at Newcastle. Why don't you ride over that way right now?"

The man's hand moved for his holster, but ten rifles raised in unison by the survey party stopped him short.

"Okay, okay, so we are out to raise a little hell, what's wrong with that?"

Gillette shook his head, smiled and walked away. "Nothing, except you ought to do it where it'll do you some good."

One shot was fired straight into the air and the ten rifles bristled again, on the edge of a miniature range war.

The tall rider yelled at the backrider who fired the shot and the gang backed horses, wheeled and disappeared over a rise.

The hair on the back of Brag's neck settled down, but his hands shook and he hid them in his pockets.

Was everybody in Wyoming Territory pissed off at the railroad? He wondered if it would ever get as far as a shooting war.

Gillette called his party together that night. "Men, you'll be delighted to know we're all going home for Christmas. Home, that is, to Crawford. I don't have to tell you how well you've done your jobs and how pleased I am that we've avoided any difficulties so far. Tomorrow, we'll pack the camp, head back to end-of-track and ride the pay train back to Crawford.

"Brag, wire Day and tell him we're coming in for Christmas."

It was the best news Brag had heard in a long time.

The party retraced its steps back along the route they had surveyed during the past five, hard months. Brag was amazed that the road gangs were only ten miles behind them. The pay train, coming out once a month, awaited them behind the work train.

Brag thought ahead. How much time would he have in Crawford? How would Elly greet him? Had she found someone else there? The thoughts zipped through his mind like a dozen bullets, ricocheting across his mind.

First, he must develop a stronger relationship with Townsend. It was best to get on good terms with him first, and then Jennie, too.

He was 25, gainfully employed by a reputable railroad, pioneering its way west, and Brag suspected that would be important in Townsend's mind. He certainly wasn't the kind of roughneck found in frontier towns like Crawford. And, hadn't they struck up a good relationship, albeit a short one, on the trip out?

The train covered the nearly one-hundred miles to Crawford in less than three hours. The town was already lit up with premature Christmas cheer, as were most of its inhabitants.

Brag checked into the hotel where a note from Elly awaited. The Townsends would appreciate his presence at their home for supper as soon as he returned. Obviously, Day had informed the townspeople that Gillette and his party would be home for Christmas.

"Welcome back and Merry Christmas," Day said when Brag walked in the door. "You did a swell job out there and you got a raise, straight from Omaha."

It was the first in a string of Christmas presents Brag was to receive the next few days.

The Townsends lived in the first permanent, respectable house in town, unlike the clapboard and tarpaper shacks that made up most of the town. It was a short hike from the depot, up the dusty main street, yet without a name.

"Well, hello, Brag," Townsend said, firmly shaking his hand at the door. "Welcome home and a Merry Christmas."

"The same to you, sir."

Then Elly appeared.

"Happy Christmas, Brag," Elly said, taking his hand and leading him into the living room. Jennie, greeted him with a handshake and kiss on the cheek.

He was dazzled by the change in Elly. She seemed taller, more mature and certainly more enchanting. Of course, he thought, it had been months since he'd seen her and, naturally, there would be changes. But, she was more beautiful than he remembered.

Elly was nearly as tall as Brag, who stood a good six feet. She was slender, yet not a twig, with a marvelous fair complexion, gorgeous hazel eyes and deep, auburn hair. She carried herself proudly, accented by the gentle sweep of her neck into high cheekbones and a classic nose. Looking at Jennie, Brag saw the resemblance immediately.

Elly also possessed another Townsend trait, she was proud. He sat next to her on the divan, breathing in her essence and trying not to act like the country oaf.

"How were your days in the field, Brag?" she asked, her slender fingers curling around his.

"Oh, they went very well. It was quite an education out there with Mr. Gillette. He's one of the strongest men I've ever known."

Elly smiled. "Yes, my father has known him ever since the Denver and the Rio Grande. My father has a business in Denver, too, you know?"

When she smiled, her eyes smiled, too, flecks of darker hazel blazing in the pupils. He felt an electricity between them and he began to sweat.

"We did have a grand time, though, what with all the excitement," he hinted.

"Oh, you saw Indians?"

"No. Some range riders came into camp one day and threatened to shoot us off the land. Mr. Gillette was cool, though. He handled it just like he was expecting it."

"But, did you ever see an Indian? We hear that they are all around, but I've only seen one occasionally in town."

He shifted in his seat and found comfort in studying her face. She caught him staring, blushed and looked down.

"There's a Christmas dance down at the town hall and we are going," she revealed suddenly. "Are you going?"

"No. First I've heard of it."

"Well, maybe we'll meet you there. It promises to be a lot

of fun and all the town big-wigs will be there, plus any number of pretty girls, too." She waited for an answer and, when none came, got up and moved toward the dining table.

Damn, maybe I should ask her, Brag thought. Maybe it's too late now. And, anyway, I don't have a decent suit to wear.

He followed her into the dining room where the Townsends were gathered with about twenty fashionably dressed townsfolk. He was in rare company and felt uncomfortable. He knew it would be impolite to cut and run, so he began to wander.

Suddenly, Elly was at his side, took his arm and walked him back into the dining room.

"I'd like you to meet some of father's friends."

In fact, some of his friends were actually town competitors, including the proprietor of Paxton & Gallaher of Omaha, in the same retail business as Townsend. The town mayor, sheriff and several other businessmen were there, along with their wives.

Elly introduced him with easy grace and he shook hands with them all.

"See, that wasn't so bad, was it?" she said softly as she moved him off into a corner. "I can see you aren't comfortable unless you are surrounded by a thousand acres of empty prairie."

Her observation startled him, more so because she was absolutely correct. He was nervous in such high-grade company and, considering he had met no one more powerful than Mr. Farswell and Gillette, he thought he handled it pretty well.

"Do you know, Brag, you have the same color eyes I have? And, that you tend to stare at people, especially me. No, don't deny it. I've felt it and seen it, too."

He was flattered and surprised.

"Well, yes, I like to look into people's souls, if you really want to know the matter of it." He was joking and she grasped it immediately.

She laughed, the delicate ring of tiny bells, then said, "Are you a deep person, Brag? I mean, do you stare because you are dissecting people? Are you dissecting me?"

It was his turn to laugh. Their conversation had progressed to a more comfortable level and he was beginning to enjoy it.

"Let's go into the garden," Elly volunteered.

He took her arm, she snuggled close and they walked away from the crowd into the garden. The sun dipped below the hills, its rays searching the garden with golden fingers.

"Oh, it's so lovely out here," she said. "I thought of you often when you were gone, Brag. I often wished I could be out there with you. I'm a city girl by birth, although you might not know that Camp Grove is a small town in Illinois. I'm eighteen now, but I've traveled a lot. My father's business takes him all over, you see. What does your father do?"

"My father and mother are sharecroppers in Ohio," he answered with hesitation. She didn't blink an eye.

"Oh, how wonderful. Do you have any brothers or sisters?"

"Yes I have three sisters and six brothers. How about you?"

"I have a twin sister still living in Camp Grove and she's not married."

She glanced at him and the corners of her mouth turned up in a smile. "But, how did you get along with so many in your family? Did you have a hard time of it?"

They sat now on a white, wrought-iron bench and Elly proceeded to pull from him things he hadn't mentioned or even thought about since leaving Ohio.

"Well, we made do with what we had," he said. "We had a great friend in my brother-in-law, John Berry. He is married to one of my sisters. He's a solicitor in Cincinnati. Got plenty of money. He is very good to our family, I think because he likes my father so well. He's the one who got me the job on the Q."

"Did you like your father, too, Brag?"

"No, as a matter of fact. I sort of ran away from him." He then told her the whole story and could tell she was interested.

They held hands as he talked and she frequently brushed

his cheek with a finger. When he finished, her eyes sparkled and she was bursting to talk.

"It's all so wonderful. I mean, you working so hard there, getting through the school and earning a job out here so far away from home. Do you ever get homesick? I do."

"No, there is so many exciting things going on out here and I have so many things to look forward too. I'm really just getting started, but I think I have a great future out here."

"Is marriage in your future?" she said boldly. He smiled and looked away.

"I don't know, but would I be forward if I said that if I were to get married, you would be my first choice?"

She threw her head back and laughed.

"You mean you have other choices?"

They laughed.

Just then, Jennie appeared.

"Oh, there you are. We're serving now if you can tear yourselves away from each other. Did you enjoy my garden, Brag?"

Brag had heard stories about the extravagant lifestyles of some of the western wealthy, bringing a new elitism to the raw west and its uncivilized towns at end-of-track.

The Townsends outdid even the tallest camp tale.

The menu Brag was handed as he sat at the huge table was a book of foreign words.

"What's Pheasant Edouard Herriot?" he whispered to Elly sitting very near him.

"Pheasants, walnut oil, truffles, mushrooms and crayfish," she whispered back with a smile.

Then, after the blessing, Jennie spoke up. "We've tried all kinds of Christmas dinners before, seafood, wild game, traditional turkey and cooked them American style. Lately, though, we've gotten more into continental cooking. I hope you all enjoy it."

Brag discovered later that the Townsends had their own cook, a former head chef at a prime Boston restaurant.

With the pheasant, Christmas Eve dinner included Black

Forest braised venison, tomato bouillon, Yorkshire pudding, Lyonnaise carrots, celery cabbage salad and jellied plum pudding.

"There is more," Jennie declared, then proceeded to run down a list of tantalizing treats for Christmas dinner the next day. They included traditional turkey with mushroom and oyster stuffing, sherried sweet potato souffle, broccoli, a green salad bowl and individual plum puddings with Brazil-nut hard sauce.

Jennie was in her heaven, gloriously entertaining. "We shall have side dishes, too." She included hot and cold cuts of turkey, roast beef, venison and pheasant, nuts, fruits, greens, candies and cakes.

The Townsends' warm hospitality, the extravagance of their Christmas holidays and being so close to Elly the next two weeks was heady wine for Brag. He was with her daily during the 'tween week and they partied well into the New Year's morning.

"It's been just glorious being with you," Elly said as they sat in the garden trying to shake their hangovers.

"I hate to see you go back out there. I'll miss you greatly."

"And I will miss you more than you know," he responded. He hugged her close, kissed her cheeks, her eyes, her lips. She returned his warmth with equal fervor.

Then, he realized he was in love for the first time in his life.

Cattle Rustlers?

Brag and Elly set their wedding date for May 17, 1890. It promised to be the most festive event since the railroad hit town. Winfield Scott Townsend would see to that.

Gillette and his crew, however, faced a huge task the next five months before Brag could return for the big day.

The big-wigs of the Burlington, the Grand Island & Northern Wyoming and Burlington & Missouri River railroads met at Townsend's store the day after New Year's Day to map out their next push.

Gillette and his crew were there. Burlington's president, Charles E. Perkins, chaired the meeting and laid out the strategy. A number of deadlines must be met, most importantly the Montana terminus by sometime in 1894. That gave the GI&NW four years to cover the almost three-hundred miles to its hook-up with the Northern Pacific at Huntley, Montana.

The Q would move its northwestern headquarters from Crawford to Sheridan, nearly two-hundred miles closer to Billings.

Newcastle had grown up suddenly, not unlike other railroad towns in the past. It now had the KB&C commissary, a drug store, a meat market, a hardware store and even a dry goods and clothing store. The Q built its hotel and yards there and Cambria's rich coal deposits provided all the fuel it would need on its push north and west.

Perkins said there was talk all across the territory that statehood was very near for Wyoming. Montana had been a state for two months now. He emphasized that territorial status for Wyoming came primarily through the building of the Union Pacific Railroad. He wanted the Burlington to be the impetus for statehood.

He also outlined the goals of the B&M: Open up cattle country and the revenue that cattle shipping could bring; tap the resources of Powder River, Crazy Woman Creek and Clear Creek on the free public range east of the Big Horn Mountains; tap the vast coal deposits known to be in these valleys, and make connection with the Northern Pacific at Huntley to give the Burlington a throughway to the Pacific.

"We have a great opportunity here, gentlemen," Perkins concluded. "The Burlington & Missouri Railroad, right from its gandy dancers to its administrators, must put forward all effort to complete this task on time. Up to now, Burlington crews have laid more than seven-thousand miles of track across this great land. There are golden rewards out there for everyone who puts his nose to the grindstone."

The speech reinforced Brag's feeling that he was hooked up to the right outfit and that his future was bright. That was especially important, now that he was to be wed.

The meeting broke up and the participants adjourned to the nearest saloon. The celebration that followed came so close to the Townsends' New Year's bash that it took very little to tip Brag into the unconscious. He woke up the next morning on a cot in the bar's back room with Jimmy shaking him awake.

"Mr. Gillette wants to see us all at the section house," Jimmy declared.

What Gillette said barely penetrated Brag's foggy mind.

"We are moving, lock, stock and barrel, to Newcastle tomorrow," Gillette began. "As Mr. Perkins says, it's back to the grindstone, boys."

Brag hurried over to the Townsends, met Elly at the door and took her into the garden.

"We're leaving tomorrow and I don't know when I'll see you again," he said. "I only know that I will miss you very much."

She embraced him.

"Yes, me too. But, you have a most important date in five months. That will be five months too long without you."

"Yes, Mr. Gillette of course knows the date and he will get us back here on time, come hell or high water."

Elly walked him to the door, they kissed and Brag anchored the look of her firmly in his mind.

Day loaded Brag with more equipment, including a new key and relay, fresh batteries and updated manuals.

"Good luck and keep up the good work," he said.

The move was completed with much less effort than Brag would have thought. Horses, mules, wagons, foodstuffs, tents and other equipment were loaded aboard stock cars and railed to Newcastle and then beyond to end of track at Moorcroft. The road gangs and rail crews had taken a shorter holiday break and were already back on the job. All together, about 186 men and their equipment and stock were moved.

It was quite a thrill for Brag as the train rolled over new rails he helped build. The scenery was as familiar to him as his code books. Off to the north, Brag spotted Devil's Tower, an awesome pillar of stone which was to become the first national monument. One day, Brag thought, he would have to ride over to the tower and peer up at its great stone height.

Gillette took the crew to end-of-track, then marched them twenty miles over already surveyed ground before pitching camp.

They would start surveying the next morning, following the general northwest run of Iron and Coyote Creeks.

Gillette had sent out advance parties in the past months, led by three Crow scouts who had worked for Custer, to map out a tentative route to Sheridan.

It was nearly two hundred miles to Sheridan, through the Belle Fourche and Powder River Valleys over rolling hills and relatively flat prairie. The advance parties were waiting for Gillette.

"It looks good," they told Gillette. "The scouts know the country well and there are several routes that look very feasible."

Brag stood by when Gillette called his crew together that night and mapped out the next day's survey.

"We'll break up into two-man crews, each taking these routes," he said, drawing his finger along the new map sketches. "Brag, you and Tom take this compass heading here. The rest of us will fan out. We can cover a lot of territory that way and hopefully, we won't miss an easy route. I don't have to tell you to take frequent compass headings and make your sketches as accurate as possible. Be back here in five days."

Tom would do the sketches and Brag would provide the compass readings. Tom Blake was the party's transitman and an inveterate practical joker. A smile always seemed to brighten his angular face and he threw his lanky body into his tasks with fierce vigor. His jokes were raw and funny and he was the best artist in the party.

Good weather had blessed the party since Brag had joined, but when they awoke the next morning before dawn, the smell of snow was in the air.

"We're in for a real blow," Tom said as they loaded the mules and checked their equipment. "Better take all the warm gear you've got, Brag."

Wyoming winters were notoriously wicked. Thousands of

cattle, horses and men had perished in terrible blizzards the past two winters. Indians, Army scouts and cowboys riding herd still came across the frozen and decayed bodies of men and cattle, lost in the blinding ground blizzards.

Ominous gray clouds scurried low across the sky from the Big Horn Mountains a hundred miles to the west as the parties set out on their routes. The rising sun was barely perceptible and its sick, yellow glow gave off little warmth.

Brag and Tom mounted their two big geldings, looped the mule leads around their saddle horns and headed out of Moorcroft, watching the other men split off and disappear into the hills.

Brag thought of Elly as they rode. May seemed an eternity away and much could happen between now and their marriage. He wondered how he could support her, buy a house, food and other essentials, all on forty-five dollars a month. He was sure Townsend would help set them up, but he was unsure whether he wanted to accept his help. That would be a handout and he wasn't sure how Elly would react if he accepted. One of the reasons he wanted out of Feesburg and away from his father was independence. He would make it on his own, no matter the circumstances, no matter his marriage, no matter what challenges awaited them.

He followed Tom as he picked his way along a buffalo trail on the spine of a low ridge. Brag could see Tom was an accomplished horseman by the way he urged the pinto along, never hard on the reins and allowing the horse to pick the easiest going. They were about ten miles out of Moorcroft and it was getting colder.

After they topped another ridge, Tom dismounted, unpacked his sketch material and set up camp.

"We've got a good view back along our trail from here, so I'd better sketch it in," Tom noted. "You better rustle up some cold grub. I wouldn't start a fire, the wind's really picking up."

Brag opened a can of beans, laid out a couple of strips of venison jerky and a canteen of cold tea. Even though there wasn't an Englishman in the party, Brag was amazed how much tea the men drank. He discovered they liked it for its flavor and kick and they could enjoy it cold. Coffee, however, was the preferred drink at hot camps.

He watched as Tom sketched the hills, gullies, creeks and spotty clumps of low vegetation. He worked meticulously and Brag was amazed how quickly his pencil drew in the details with remarkable accuracy.

"How do they name the towns along the railroad?" Brag asked, out of the blue.

Tom eyed down his outstretched pencil tip to get a measure, then smiled. "Most of the towns are named after local cattlemen, politicians or railroad men. Some towns are already there and we use them as guide posts along the route. Most, though, spring up when the railroad arrives, then often disappear as quickly when folks don't settle there. Most folks have wanderlust. I'm sure that's what brought you out here, right, Brag?"

He went on, not waiting for an answer.

"Most folks nowadays are looking for greener pastures. Most folks nowadays don't find greener pastures until they are buried under one. Lots of folks dying on the way out here, folks dying when they get here and folks dying heading on west. It makes no difference, really. We're all going under our own little plot of earth somewhere, sometime or another.

"Just seems a waste of good folks for them not to be settling in somewhere quickly and living out a full life. No sense wandering under a star all your life."

Brag was delighted. His simple question had brought surprising philosophy from an unexpected source.

"You a wanderer, Tom?"

"Was once, for the longest time."

Tom was finished now, packed up his gear and sat down to eat.

"Wandered all over the East. I was born in Minnesota and went to work for the Burlington years ago, when I was just a kid." He smiled and Brag sensed that one of Tom's ribald jokes was next. But, instead, he talked about his new wife,

Bertha, and their new homestead just outside Cambria.

"Yep, done a lot of years for the Q up till now, but I'm not burned out yet. As a matter of fact, got a joke about long-time work for a company."

His smile grew broader and, without hesitation, he told it.

"Seems a Negro porter had worked for Burlington almost since the day it reached St. Paul. He loved folks, loved his job working the coach cars and loved the travel.

"One day, the Q bought a whole slew of them new Pullman sleeper cars and this Negro was assigned to work one on the overnight run between Minneapolis-St. Paul and points west. Well, he didn't like them new-fangled cars one bit, no sir, not one bit. He said he was too old to learn new tricks and considered the Pullman was a trick on the passengers.

"Tricked passengers into buying tickets because they offered comfort and ease, he'd say. Tricked 'em because they thought sleeping overnight on a train was the best thing since buttered bread, and it wasn't. He told his superiors that, unless they gave him back his old job, he'd quit.

"Well, they didn't, and he did."

"But, what's the joke?" Brag asked.

"Know what he did?"

Brag shook his head.

"That old Negro signed on with the Northern Pacific as a Pullman porter. He works Pullmans across the same tracks used by the Burlington. Ain't that irony?"

The blizzard struck almost without warning. Tom saw the wall of snow moving in from the north, a low menacing sheet of white swirling over the hills and down through the draws.

"Grab the horses and mules!" he shouted. "Get them down in that gully and get them hobbled as fast as you can! It's going to blow bad!" Tom exclaimed.

Within seconds, they were nearly blown flat by a howling wind driving snow almost horizontally. The flakes stung their faces like grains of sand as they fought to control the horses and mules. Finally, Tom got both horses on the ground by throwing blankets over their heads. The mules, tied to the saddles, stubbornly refused to go down and turned their tails to the blast.

"If I know my Wyoming ground blizzards, there's clear sky a hundred feet above us," Tom shouted through the screaming wind.

All they could do was drag blankets out of saddlebags and huddle against the horses. Fortunately, they were in a gully and Brag could see the wind and snow ripping across the summit of the hill, just like a sheet shaking in the wind. Still, enough wind ripped into the gully to pile snow against them and soon they were nearly buried. It was just as well for it seemed to shelter them from the cold.

"Glad we got down here," Tom yelled. "We'd have been blown clear off that ridge by now and the horses scattered. If I know anything, I know my Wyoming winters."

Brag shook his head and snuggled closer against the horse's belly. Its warmth invaded him, but soon rivulets of water ran down into his clothes as the snow melted against the steaming horse.

The storm blew itself out an hour later and a bright sun burned off the last shattered cloud.

They stood up, shook off the snow and looked around. The wall of white was headed east now and all around them the land bore a soft, new blanket of snow. Brag had been through blizzards before, but this one showed a fury he never thought possible.

"Well, not as bad as some I've been through," Tom exclaimed.

They pulled the horses out and climbed to the top of the ridge.

Brag figured the snow blanket would be deeper, but the wind had cleared the summits of the ridges. Each stood out brown and sparse while the gullies were buried. It looked like someone had smeared fingers across the white frosting on a chocolate cake. The sky was high and crystal clear all the way to the Big Horns.

"Gillette and the other parties are in for it, too," Tom

noted, looking east at the retreating storm. "But, they are all old storm veterans and they'll ride it out, too."

"Are we going on?" Brag inquired.

"Sure. The snow's not as deep as it looks and we'll stick to the ridge tops," Tom replied. "We've still got work to do."

The going was slower as the horses carefully picked their way over hidden ground. They surveyed another ten miles with Tom adding to his pile of sketches.

"It was a good storm. Didn't bury us and it gives me a look at where the snow drifts in the gullies and ridges," Tom noted.

"Often, we lay a line through on a supposedly good route, only to find out later that we have to build snow fences. Fences are expensive and time-consuming, so we try to avoid them."

The weather held the next four days, a warm sun burning off the snow that filled the gullies with little, muddy streams. The horses seemed to enjoy the long day's work, but the mules were in their usual cantankerous moods.

They had surveyed about twenty miles north and west of Moorcroft up along Buffalo Creek and Tom suggested they take a more westerly route going back. That way, they could cover new ground.

Day and night, Elly's image never left Brag's mind. He put together a calendar of the days that would follow their wedding. They would find a house in Newcastle or Cambria, settle in and begin raising a family. Elly had said she wanted a big family. She said she missed the warmth and joy she had seen in larger families.

"I'd like a whole bunch of kids, maybe five boys and five girls," she told him.

He shook his head and laughed to himself. It was a grim thought, though, all those mouths to feed on his meager salary. Still and all, he came from a large family and understood why Elly would want such a large brood. He remembered the look of joy in his mother's face as she struggled to feed him and his brothers and sisters. It was something Brag would like to see in Elly's face, too. Yet, there were other more practical problems to consider.

Two days out from Moorcroft, another range gang found them at evening camp.

"Howdy. Coffee?" Brag offered, following the same coolness he'd seen in Gillette.

"Yep, could use some," the dismounted rider said. Two others joined him at the fire. All were lightly dressed, like they'd come from a ranch not too far off.

"You railroad surveyors?" the second, stocky man asked.

"Yea, working for the B&M toward Montana," Tom replied, eyeing them with suspicion.

"We heard that the railroad was coming through, but we didn't realize you were this far along," the first man declared.

Brag suspected they might be part of the larger gang which had confronted them earlier, and he wanted to know more.

"How come all you ranger riders in this particular part of Wyoming are so interested in our railroad?" Brag asked and waited for a reaction.

The man's face tightened and he spat his words out underneath a grease-stiff moustache. "We want to know where you're getting your beef?"

"Who the hell are you?" Tom shot back.

"We're from the YT Ranch over on Salt Creek and Mr. Hunter wants to know why your railroad crews are stealing our cattle."

It was the first time Brag or Tom had heard any such thing. Pierre shot wildlife and trapped for the Gillette crew and any beef the crew got came by rail from Newcastle. As far as either of them knew, Pierre never brought beef to their camp fires.

"We don't know anything about beef. You say we're rustling your brand?" Brag wanted to know.

All three men stood up and squared off, shoulder to shoulder, hands on hips. Brag's Remington was slung on his horse and Tom didn't have a sidearm.

"No, we're not accusing anybody, but Mr. Hunter has been losing stock the past few weeks and we've been sent out to find them," the shortest of the three replied. He was broad and beefy with a fleshy face and haggard look. "We found a few strays just north of here, then saw your camp. We're checking all possible sources."

"Well, you can be sure we don't have beef, in this outfit, anyway," Tom said. "We've been cold camping on venison jerky and beans for days now. But, we'd sure appreciate a side if you happen to have one along."

Tom wouldn't let the sticky situation inhibit his sense of humor. "Yes sir, sure could stand a sizzling steak right now."

Hard looking as they were, Tom's reply seemed to disarm the men.

"Well, I suspect the two of you ain't got the wherewithal to steal a beef, anyway," the fat man said. "But, we would sure like to hear about it if you run across any rustlers."

With that, the men mounted and rode off without a look back.

"Wonder why they think we'd be rustlers?" Brag asked.

"It's been going on for a while now, ever since Stuart and his Stranglers did in some rustlers up in Montana some years back," Tom said. "Things have been building up around here, too. Gillette knows more about it than I do, but he's said that there's bound to be a range war before it's all over."

They broke camp and in two days were back in Moorcroft.

The Wedding

Three-quarters of the population of Crawford greeted Brag and the survey party at the station that bright, cool May morning and Elly was first in line.

"Welcome home, Brag." She kissed him long and hard and clung close as they moved to their carriage.

She was never more beautiful, dressed in bright yellow with a matching parasol and wide-brimmed white hat bedecked with live flowers. The image of her he had carried in his mind the past months vanished, replaced by one more stunning and real. Her radiance seemed to dominate the scene and her eyes communicated a love he couldn't recall seeing before.

Mayor Frank Jeremy strode up, shook Brag's hand and kissed Elly. "Our town is indeed fortunate to have such fine, young upstanding citizens whose future looks as bright as that of Crawford's," he said, somewhat pompously and, as it turned out, not totally correct.

Their carriage led a parade of well-wishers down the street to the hotel where Brag would prepare for the grand prenuptial celebration that night at the community hall on the hill.

By the looks of it, Crawford's residents had found still another, albeit more legitimate, excuse for a party and were well into their cups even before the actual wedding the next afternoon.

Brag couldn't wait to get Elly to the hotel, forcing his way through the crowd which greeted them as they alighted from their carriage. Jennie whispered that it would not be proper for Elly to go to Brag's room, a two-room suite more spacious than his room across the street. Townsend had made all the arrangements.

"You wait here, Elly, I'll bathe and change and be right down," Brag said as he escorted her into the crowded sitting room. She smiled and kissed him fervently.

"Hurry."

Gillette and the crew somehow had beaten him to his room and were already riding high. Jake, Tom, Mike, Joe and Pierre and even Judy, their camp dog, were there.

A huge bar had been set up and a clothes rack in one corner held countless new shirts, pants, suits and ties. Fresh changes were laid out on the bed, but weren't getting fresher with the press of Tom's butt sitting broadly on them.

"Pour yourself a stiff one, Brag, and we'll drink the first of many toasts to you and Elly," Gillette commanded. The whiskey burned a fiery trace into his belly and rebounded to his head.

"Don't any of you have homes, wives?" Brag questioned. He knew most of them did, and he was delighted that they showed such affection by being here after five months away.

"Sure, and we'll be going real soon, too, soon as we drink all that up," Tom responded with a wild wave toward the bar.

Gillette brought the party to a halt. "No, Brag, we're

leaving now. You have to get ready and we have to get home. We'll see you at the reception later."

Brag changed, finding that the new pants were too long and the coat too short, but comfortable and hardly noticeable.

He quickly found Elly surrounded by well-wishers and they shared a drink before Townsend spirited them out the door, into the carriage and away to their house. It was obvious Townsend had something on his mind and wanted to confront Brag as soon as possible.

"Now, tell me, son, where do you plan to settle?" was Townsend's first question as they sat in the expansive drawing room. "You don't mind if I call you son, for soon you will be?" Brag read the affection in his eyes.

The Townsends had never had a son, and it was obvious that Townsend seemed to cherish having one in the family, albeit not of blood.

"Well, we're northwest of Moorcroft now and it looks like we'll be working there for a spell, anyway. I'd as soon settle in Cambria if it's okay with Elly."

Townsend handed him another drink, paused, then said, "Okay, but you play hell to find a decent house on your pay. I suppose you could homestead, though."

He walked nervously across the room, fixed himself another drink, then continued. "I don't know how you feel about some help from our direction. We're not the wealthiest folks in this town, but I do get some monthly stock dividends and Nash Finch pays pretty well.

"I'm sure you know by now how difficult it is for a man and his family to make a go of it out here, what with the drought, the silver situation and the country's financial straits."

"Yes, sir, I do know that." Brag suddenly felt a warm kinship with Townsend. Certainly, he had Brag's interests at heart and, since he soon would give up his daughter to him, held a more than passing interest in their future.

Townsend was right about one thing, it wasn't going to be easy getting his family started.

"Gillette said he would help us find something up there

and I have a few contacts, too, through the telegraph office," Brag continued. "They are still building new houses in Cambria as the miners keep flooding in and there are homestead plats around there, too."

"Have you saved any money?"

"Yes, sir, I've put back about two hundred dollars, some of what Berry gave me, some from my salary. I got a five-dollar raise last month, but I know it isn't much. Seems like fifty dollars a month doesn't go very far nowadays."

Townsend pulled up a chair and sat close to Brag. "That's all well and good, Brag, but I want you to listen for a minute to what I have to say.

"I know the situation here in Wyoming probably better than you do," he started. "You've been out in the boondocks the past few months and out of touch."

Brag studied Townsend as he spoke. He was a tall, slender man with an aristocratic air about him, yet without conceit or vanity. He was handsome, Brag concluded, and he could see much of Elly in his facial characteristics. Confidence emanated from him.

"Here's what I've done for my soon-to-be son-in-law and my precious daughter," Townsend said, drawing Brag back to reality. "I've set aside several thousand dollars in a fund for Elly and you. I have not attached stipulations or conditions to your use of that fund, but I would expect you to use your head in its expenditure. Jennie and I also have been house-hunting, in both Newcastle and Cambria."

He poured them another drink and that seemed to relax the tension Brag saw in his face. He guessed that Townsend found the situation somewhat difficult to present.

"Wait a minute, sir," Brag interjected. "You mean Elly and I already have a substantial bank account, thanks to you?"

"That's the jist of it, I guess. It's not out of the ordinary for a father to want the best for his daughter and, dammit, out here the best is not only hard to find, it's downright expensive."

Brag stood up and moved across the room, his mind wrestling with the situation. What Townsend was offering was a naked handout, but in such a gracious way that Brag couldn't refuse.

"Does Elly know about this?" he asked.

"Yes, Brag, as a matter of fact, she's the one who proposed it. She said it would be her dowry. I would call it, more accurately, her hope chest."

Brag could see Townsend was uncomfortable.

"Very well, then, sir, you can count on us to be very frugal with that money and I thank you very much for the trust you put in me."

The anxiety fell from Townsend's face and he embraced Brag.

"Good, now let's get on to the reception."

Crawford's community hall was the largest place in town that could accommodate the many relatives and friends expected for the reception and wedding. It was one of the first structures built after the railroad hit town and some care was taken in its construction.

The hall was booming when Brag and the Townsends arrived. Gillette, Brag's best man, and the whole crew were there with their wives and girlfriends. Members of the Knights of Pythias, resplendent in their white pith helmets, belts and gloves, mingled with the crowd of about two hundred. Cambria miners were easily distinguishable by their rough dress and pallid complexions. The mayor and town council gathered in a group, no doubt discussing politics. The town band, a cross-section of citizens, played loudly, and off key, in one corner. The town's fire brigade was in uniform, as was the town baseball team, fresh from a victory over the Cambria miners that afternoon.

It was a splendid scene, Brag thought, as he escorted Elly to the bar.

The reception line soon formed and Brag, Elly and the Townsends were busy shaking hands and greeting the many guests. First in line was the mayor, followed by the councilmen, the sheriff and the fire and police chiefs. Gillette and his party were next, then Day shook his hand, then Jimmy and on and on. The parade seemed endless.

Finally, Townsend stepped forward, quieted the hall with a wave of his hand, and proposed a toast. "Here's to the happy couple. May they find continued peace and happiness and infinite success."

Then, the townsfolk presented a small collection of gifts to Elly and Brag. Most were very practical. A washboard and tub, aprons, silverware, linen and cooking pots for Elly. Day gave Brag a new model telegraph key, Gillette presented a new bridle and Tom, ever the jokester, presented him with a new shovel.

"It's to dig that big garden you are going to need to feed all your kids," he laughed.

The reception might have gone on all night, but Townsend called a halt about two in the morning. "We've all got to get some rest before the wedding and we'll see you back here this afternoon."

The final drink was guzzled and the hall emptied slowly as reluctant guests departed. The town was unusually quiet that morning as the Townsend party headed home.

White was definitely Elly's color Brag thought as he escorted her down the aisle of people in the hall that bright May afternoon. She was his dream come true. Her auburn hair and hazel eyes were a beautiful contrast to her white lace veils and flowing gown.

They took the vows from the notary, kissed and turned to face the bleary-eyed crowd. Elly wanted as many friends and folks as possible at her wedding so she chose the town hall. Later they would repeat their vows before the priest in a private ceremony at the town church.

The reception that followed was, by necessity, shorter and less boisterous. The party goers were partied out and most of the folks had to return to work.

Gillette shook Brag's hand once again. "You've got a couple of days off now, Brag, but we'll be shoving off then. The grading crews have nearly caught us and there's work to be done."

Elly and Brag would remain with the Townsends until they could find a place in Newcastle or Cambria. Townsend said that housing in Newcastle was limited even though many new houses were being built. Elly, however, wanted to move quickly and the situation in Cambria was more promising.

Brag had doubts. "I'm not sure we'd like to live in a mining town," he noted. "I've met some of those men and they're a pretty wild bunch."

"I know, but the town council didn't allow a single saloon there," Townsend revealed. "I know that the miners have to trek on down to Newcastle to get drunk."

Brag had heard rumors to that effect and what Townsend said pretty much decided that they would hunt for a place in Cambria. He decided his two days off would be better spent house-hunting there than with Elly, reluctant as he was to leave her.

"It seems like we're saying good-bye all the time," she said when told of his decision. "I just hope this isn't going to be a terrible habit with us."

He looked at her and shook his head. "Elly, dear, the nature of my job is such that I will be out in the boondocks for long stretches. So, I'll not be saying good-bye too often, but will be long times between our good-byes." He laughed and took her in his arms, afraid she might cry.

"Oh, I understand. It's just that here we are, newly married, and I haven't even slept in the same bed with you yet. Do you suppose we could manage that before you leave?"

Brag was not surprised. From the first moment they met, Brag had a hint of latent sensuality there, a fleeting glimpse of a longing yet to be fulfilled.

"You are right," he exclaimed. "And, by God, we'll do so. It might be somewhat embarrassing for your folks, don't you think?"

She laughed and snuggled closer. "Oh, I think it would be all right. After all, Mother has talked to me often about such matters and Daddy is totally unabashed about such things." She laughed and Brag caught an air of recklessness in her laugh.

"You know, that during our time together, our love has

progressed through stages, like the building of our railroad," Brag declared.

"First, we sort of 'surveyed' each other. Then, we mentally sketched out plans to show our love, in one way or another. Finally, our love had reached a stage where the roadbed was put down, that was our wedding. Now, the rails must be laid that point to our future."

She smiled at his graphic simile, then said something even more graphic. "The rails aren't the only thing that must be laid, Brag."

They both laughed. Her bluntness surprised him and so did her eagerness to consummate their marriage. Brag never imagined Elly to be so aware of sex, coming as she did from a very upright, conservative family. He wondered if she was still a virgin.

Suddenly, she snuggled close, kissing his lips with a hot fervor he had never felt before.

Jennie walked in.

"Well, the newlyweds aren't wasting any time, are they?" she said without a blush. "If you hurry, you'll find the upstairs bedroom vacant and I can stall the maids down here. Winfield is downtown."

She laughed as Elly jumped up, blushing.

"Sorry, Mrs. Townsend. We were just discussing our future," Brag stammered.

"Well, I'd say much of it lies within the scope of what you two were about to do." She patted Brag on the shoulder, winked at Elly and walked out of the room.

"You see, Brag, Mother's no prude. Do you want to go upstairs?"

They dashed up the stairs and into each other's arms in the nearest bedroom.

"I want you. I've wanted you from that first day I saw you," she said.

Brag caressed her face, then pulled her down and kissed her urgently. She responded, but he could feel a tenseness in her body.

"I love you very much, Elly," he whispered, "probably more than you'll ever know."

"Yes, I felt your love whenever you looked at me, and I just knew we would be together soon," she responded, her breath coming in gasps.

He tentatively grasped her breast through her dress, and felt her body tense again.

"You've never done this before?" he asked.

"No, have you?"

"No this is a first time for me, too."

She pushed him away, stared into his eyes, and asked, "You mean you're twenty-five years old and you're still a virgin, too?"

Elly had answered his unspoken question with one of her own. Again, he was not surprised.

"I supposed, that since you came from a such a large family so close to the earth, that you would know about such things?" she suggested.

The heat had suddenly died from their initial fire, reduced to mere conversation.

"Oh, of course I've seen my sisters naked often, but they are my sisters and you wouldn't expect me to be interested in them in that way, would you?"

She smiled, stroked his face and kissed him again.

"No, of course not. But, haven't you seen animals mate? Didn't you have a girl back home that was, uh, receptive to your advances?"

He laughed and hugged her so tightly she lost her breath. "How could I? I never got away from the farm long enough to make those kinds of friends or meet even the first girl. There was just no way."

She laughed. "Then, we'll just have to learn together, won't we?"

He sat up and held her at arm's length. "Where do we start, do you suppose?"

"Well, let's get our clothes off first. I think that's the first thing."

Brag watched fascinated as Elly pulled off her dress, removed her corset and underthings and sat naked on the bed.

"Come on, it's your turn now," she giggled.

It was the first time Brag had seen a woman's naked body this close, this inviting, and this available. He quickly removed his clothes. He couldn't tear his eyes away from her full, round breasts, the way her hips and stomach flowed into the triangle of dark hair between her legs.

She was staring now, at his full erection, the hard definition of his stomach and chest muscles.

"Oh, I've never seen one up close," she purred, "it's so fascinating. Can I touch it?"

Without waiting for an answer, Elly grasped him with both hands and he went weak. He responded, caressing her breasts and trailing his fingers down her body until they found the dampness between her legs. She stretched out, spreading her legs every so slightly and demurely as his fingers explored.

"Yes, and you are wonderfully fascinating, too," he whispered.

Their fondling demanded more. Brag fell into her upraised arms and their union resulted in an automatic coupling.

Brag pierced her maidenhead with his first thrusts and Elly bit her hand to suppress a scream.

He moved into her slowly at first, withdrawing, then thrusting deeply again. He felt a storm rising in his loins, then filled her with successive eruptions.

They lay exhausted. She kissed his mouth, his face, his eyelids.

"You are my first and greatest love, and for always," she exclaimed.

A terribly crude thought flashed through Brag's mind as he held her close.

One of the things the crew looked forward to around their campfire after a hard day's work were their ribald and obscene jokes. Tom's were most humorous and inexhaustible. Others in the crew told even more vulgar stories. It often seemed to Brag they were trying to top each other. Many of their jokes had to do with the "best piece of tail I ever had."

The object of their humor might have been an Indian squaw, a town whore, a pretty young farmer's daughter or even their own wives. Gillette was not a prude, but he usually called a halt if the proceedings got too raw."

Right now, Brag thought, Elly was his "best piece of tail." He smiled because she was also his first.

First Born

Jennie May was born during a fierce February blizzard in the Cooper's rented cottage above Cambria mines on the plateau known as Antelope City.

Brag couldn't get over how wrinkled and pink she was. Elly just laughed. "All babies are born like that if they're healthy," she said.

"But, she has blue eyes and no hair. I don't have blue eyes and neither do you. No one in my family does."

Elly laughed again. "Boy, for a man from a big family, you sure don't know much about babies. Many babies have blue eyes until the pigment settles. As for hair, she'll have some soon."

As he held Jennie May's tiny fingers, he pondered how such a frail thing could survive out here. He had seen calves and colts born, already miniatures of their mothers, strong and able to stand and prance only hours after birth. God only knew how long it would take Jennie May to walk and talk.

"She is a beautiful baby, though," he finally conceded.

"Brag, I'm really, really surprised you've never seen your brothers and sisters as babies. Then you'd know the answers to the questions you ask."

"Well, Sam, that's my dad, he never let us get close to mother during births. I've seen my brothers and sisters in the crib, but never too close and never too often. Sam was a stickler for that. Said we could give germs to the babies if we got close for too long."

Much had happened to Brag as 1891 moved toward the summer, most of it bad. He was pulled off the survey crew to do double duty in the Newcastle office.

The Burlington's own telephone lines were being webbed in all along the system and some telegraphers were being turned into telephone operators. Some were still needed as telegraphers, too, because code traffic was still being used station to station. The phone lines had already reached Newcastle and the linesmen were even now busy stringing new lines northwest, right on the heels of the B&M work trains.

"You're going to have to do double duty now, Brag," Day said with a chuckle. "I've hired a girl to help you work the phones and office chores, but you will still handle telegraphy to Gillette in the field."

"I just don't understand it. I've got to work now twice as hard for the same measly fifty dollars a month. I just don't understand it," Brag told Elly.

"Well, you can't resist progress, Brag," she replied. "And, besides, it's better for both of us. You'll be home with me a lot more and it's not such a bad job, is it?"

Brag shook his head. "No, it's a great job and I'm glad I have it. But, honey, it means twelve-hour days and I won't get to see that much of you."

"Well, we just have to make do with what we have," Elly

said. "After all, we're better off than most folks around here, you have to admit that." She seemed content with that and smiled at him.

"I'm not so sure," Brag said as he poured out a full glass of whiskey and gulped it down. He felt worn out, used up, and the drink pumped in a new vigor.

Elly eyed him warily. "You aren't going to start drinking on me, are you?"

He looked at her as the whiskey burned its way down. She was nursing Jennie May and her naked breast elicited no emotion in him whatever. The hell with it, he thought, maybe it will take some of the sting out of his demotion and make him feel better.

It did.

The shocks came in bunches for Brag that morning.

"There was a double murder on a homestead outside Cambria," said Day, who seemed to be forever the messenger of bad news. Then he hesitated, not sure how to break the news. "It's Tom Blake and his wife, Bertha. The whole town is up in arms."

Brag was stunned. Tom was the last person he had worked with on the survey party and he'd grown very fond him. He had never met Bertha, but Tom talked a lot about his new wife and how they looked forward to their new life in Wyoming.

"It happened two days ago, they think, but they haven't found the bodies or the murderer," Day went on. "They haven't been seen in two days."

Then, he changed the subject.

"I know you're pissed off at the Burlington and probably me, too, but I'm glad things have worked out like this for you. That's the way of it today. Still, don't you feel better being closer to Elly?"

Brag nodded his head.

"We don't know if this guy's some sort of nut, going around killing newlyweds. I don't want to take the chance with you and Elly. And, if I were you, I wouldn't mention this to Elly, either."

Brag worked the key with vengeance that day, as if pounding it would relieve his anger. He was quick and efficient receiving the daily reports from his replacement in the field, Gerry Johnson.

He couldn't get the thought out of his mind that a murderer was prowling the prairie somewhere around Cambria. Their cottage was somewhat removed from the town itself on the plateau above. It was surrounded by about forty similar cottages, all inhabited, and maybe there was a measure of protection in that. He was uneasy, though, because here in Newcastle, he was still some seven miles from Elly, alone with the new baby.

Brag's search for a house in Cambria had come up against priorities. The new mines attracted a flood of miners and their families from all over the country and Europe. They got first shot at the new houses in Cambria proper. All others had to settle in Antelope City, farther out in the prairie or down the valley. New companies were rapidly moving in and new business buildings were rising as rapidly as the sun.

If ever a town was star-crossed it was Cambria, a town just waiting to be born, thanks to the rich coal veins.

As soon as Burlington engineers determined the coal was usable, three mine shafts were dug. The Antelope Mine was tunneled into the west canyon wall and the Jumbo into the east. The third shaft was not very productive and was abandoned. A sawmill was freighted in from Alliance, since the rail line to Newcastle was not yet complete at that time. A spur rail was built seven miles down the canyon to meet the proposed Newcastle line and construction started on mine shoring, double-deck trestles, rail yard and residential and business housing.

The coal find and the subsequent stampede to the mines made Cambria a boom town while Newcastle was still a small collection of shacks. Brag had arrived in Newcastle after most of the Cambria construction was complete and the line was through.

The Kilpatrick brothers built and owned the mines and also built most of the town. Original plans called for the town on the plateau above the mines and about forty cottages were built there. However, most of the later houses were built along the valley walls nearer the mines. The first school was constructed on the plateau and the town's youngsters every day counted the three-hundred-sixty-five steps to and from the school. Later, a school was built down in the valley and the Antelope City kids had to do the climbing and counting.

A hospital was one of the first buildings constructed, soon followed by a huge men's dormitory, called the "Bull Pen." The Kilpatrick brothers strongly disapproved of drinking, so Cambria was a dry town, no saloons or gambling halls. A Saturday night beer wagon from Newcastle brought weekly relief to the miners and townsfolk. Three churches were built, as were a recreation hall and the Cambria Trading Company store.

The Cambria mines were the most modern in the country. Undercutting and drilling machinery was operated by compressed air, supplied through more than twenty miles of high-pressure pipes. Compressed air also drove the tailrope system which brought the coal out of the mines onto the tipple, and the town's water supply from deep underground.

The mines were considered the safest in the country, entirely free of explosive gases and dust with little water seepage. It was soon discovered that Cambria coal had a high coke content and seventy-five Bee Hive coke ovens were constructed along one canyon wall. The town supplied coke for the gold smelters in Deadwood and Lead, South Dakota.

Cambria also reaped an unexpected bonanza from its coal. The coal contained small quantities of gold and silver, measured out to about two dollars per ton in the coal and five dollars in the coke.

The phone rang, jarring Brag back to reality.

The girl answered, went white, and called for Day. He listened, also went white, then hung up.

"I've got more bad news for you, Brag," he said, pulling him into the outer office. "That was a friend calling for your father. Your mother has died."

Brag sank into a chair and buried his face in his hands. It

was inconceivable that Rebecca was suddenly gone. He just knew when he left her that she was not a well woman. Now, the long, hard years had finally taken their toll. Day walked away as Brag broke down and cried.

Day forced a glass full of water into his hands. "I'm sorry, Brag, so sorry," he said. "Why don't you take the rest of the day off? I won't dock you and you need it."

Brag walked slowly out of the office and sat down on the bench outside, staring blankly at the busy street.

All his world was suddenly crumbling around him. He had a new job, a new wife and a new baby. Now, he had lost part of that job, a good friend and his wife and, now, his mother. All in a day. Granted, he had written to his mother only twice in the two years he'd been out here and maybe it was his fault. Perhaps he should have stayed home. No, he couldn't have prevented her death. She was dying when he left, and she knew it. How could God be so cruel now after being so good to him? Was this the beginning of the bad times his father had warned him about?

Two short whistle blasts from the daily passenger express to Crawford broke his gloom. He had a sudden urge to run, to take that train east, to flee this land suddenly strange to him now, to retreat to a womb that was no more.

The empty glass sliced his hand as he squeezed and the blood dripped into the gray wood. He didn't feel it. Day appeared suddenly with another full glass and the girl, her face still white, wrapped his hand in a bandanna.

"Come on now, Brag, buck up," Day implored. "We'll get Jimmy to take you home and you'll feel better. Time heals all wounds."

Brag drained the glass, stood up and leaned against the porch post. His head was spinning when Jimmy appeared.

"C'mon, Mr. Brag, I'll git you back to Elly quick," Jimmy said, tugging him into the buckboard.

He didn't remember the trip home and only vaguely saw Elly's puzzled face as she greeted them at the door and got him into bed.

Then, his world went blank.

West County deputy sheriff Lee Balbo knocked on the Cooper door early the next morning.

"Hello, Mrs. Cooper, how's the new baby doing?" he asked.

"Oh, she's fine," Elly responded, wondering why he was here.

"Is Brag about?"

"Yes, but he's feeling very badly. His mother died yesterday."

"Oh, I'm sorry to hear that, Mrs. Cooper, but it's important I see him."

Elly roused Brag, who sat for a moment on the edge of the bed. "God, I feel hundred years old," he thought.

Balbo took him down the steps from the house as Elly stood on the stoop and wondered.

"We think we've found the Blakes' murderer. We think he's holed up in a shack over near Pumpkin Buttes, about seventy miles away." He paused and looked at Brag.

"You okay?"

"Yes, just too much bad news in one day."

"Well, hope you can ride because we're getting up a posse to go after him and they say you're a pretty fair rider."

"Did you talk to Mr. Day to see if it's okay that I go?"

"Yes, in fact Day wanted to go along, but he's not much of a rider and can't leave the office. You want to come? I know Tom was one of your best friends, right?"

"Yes, sure I'll go."

"Better plan on about four or five days out," Balbo said. "The PK Ranch is providing the horses, good, solid stock."

Brag rushed into the house past Elly without saying a word.

"What's going on, Brag?"

"I have to help chase down a murderer," he replied, throwing rain gear and clothes into his saddlebags and grabbing his Remington rifle.

"What murderer? Who's been killed?"

He paused at the door as Balbo waited. "I guess I better tell you or you'll fret about it while I'm gone. Tom Blake and his wife were murdered and they've cornered the murderer over near Pumpkin Buttes. They are forming a posse and I just have to go along."

"You mean Tom, the man in your survey party?"

He wanted to get going, but she kept asking questions.

"Yes, dear, that's right. They've been missing for more than three days now and they suspect foul play. I've just got to go."

"Okay, okay, but it seems to me they already have enough men to go and you're not a lawman," she insisted. "Why do you just have to go?"

"Elly, Tom Blake was my best friend," he replied impatiently. "He took me under his wing out in the boondocks and taught me all I know about this country. I've just got to go."

She kissed and hugged him, then stood back with tears in her eyes.

"Please be careful, Brag."

Balbo rode Brag double into Newcastle where about fifty men had gathered in front of the sheriff's office. Among them was Gillette, who had left his survey party far up the Wild Horse River toward Clearmont.

Townsend was standing on the steps.

"Good to see you, Brag. How's Jennie May?" he inquired.

"Good to see you, too, Mr. Townsend. She's fine."

"I reckoned you'd want to go along and I told Balbo so when he started looking for men. I hope you don't mind, Brag?"

"Not at all. I'd be pissed if I couldn't go."

Balbo gathered the dismounted men around him. "The guy we're after is Jeff Stephanic, better known as Slim around these parts," he began. "We got a tip from a friend of his in Cambria that he was bragging about killing a couple three days ago on their homestead outside Cambria.

"I know it's going to be a shock to those who knew Tom and Bertha, but we dug up their bodies late last night," Balbo revealed. He hadn't told that to Brag as they rode into town.

"This tipster told us Stephanic bragged about how he killed them, stole their horses, money and other goods, and buried them. They were shot through the head. Not a chance. They must have known Stephanic somehow or another.

"Anyway, this Stephanic was last seen riding west and this friend of his says he has other friends over near Pumpkin Buttes. It's about seventy miles there, so we'd better get riding."

One posse member wasn't so sure. "How do you know for sure this guy's where you say he is?" he shouted. "I ain't riding two hundred miles chasing a ghost!"

Balbo threw up his hands. "We aren't sure, Bill, that's where he is, but it's the only clue we have so far. I'm willing to try if all of you are too. How about it?"

The general murmur through the posse meant assent to Balbo and they mounted up, stirring up a cloud of dust as they trotted out of town.

Excitement grew in Brag. They would be traveling across new ground, and it felt great to get his body into a saddle again. Most of the posse were hard riders, cowpokes, cattle men, former Pony Express riders and cavalrymen. He might have been the novice rider of the posse, but it felt good.

It gave him an opportunity to get away from the weekly grind, from Elly and a night-bawling baby and renew his love with the open country. He relaxed, let the horse have his head and rode easily.

The posse cut across the lay of the land that ran north and south, which meant up and over many low ridges, down into dry arroyos and up again. Tough on the men, tougher on the horses. It took them three days to get to Pumpkin Buttes, standing stark in the early morning sun.

"Where to we go from here?" inquired one of the riders.

Balbo squinted through field glasses, sizing up the broken ground. "Stephanic is supposed to be holed up in a cabin somewhere near that north butte. We'll head that way after breakfast. We can stand the break."

Brag fed his horse and talked with Gillette as they ate. Gillette told him that Johnson was doing his job, but that the old crew missed Brag, missed the camaraderie they had developed over the years they were together in the field.

"It just isn't the same without you out there to keep us young," Gillette said. "But, of course, we all miss Tom very much. You know, he wanted to come back out with us again, but Bertha put her foot down. He said she told him if he ever even hinted about coming back out, she'd leave him.

"That was hard to take for a man as easy going and likeable as Tom," Gillette went on. "He told me he really did want to stay with Bertha, but that he was just joking with her about coming back out with us. He just wanted to get her bile up as a joke.

"Too bad. Now they're both gone." He shook his head, gulped the last of his coffee and stared at Brag.

"He was truly a friend of mine, perhaps the only real close friend I had out here," Brag said. "You are my friend, too, of course. But, you're the boss and that's different. Tom and I could talk about things and people like maybe I couldn't with you.

"You see, Ed, Tom was an Easterner, like me, and we seemed to understand where we both were coming from," Brag continued. He paused, wondering what Gillette was thinking.

"Tom was so funny, so easy to talk with and I didn't mind that half of his conversation was about Bertha and the other half was about getting laid."

Gillette shook his head. "Yea, I know just what you mean, Brag."

An hour's ride put the posse on a ridge overlooking a small cabin, smoke curling from its chimney. Balbo broke the posse into three parties to surround the cabin.

"Remember, men, we want this guy alive," he told them. "This is still my county jurisdiction so I'm the law out here. We'll have no lynching party or random shooting, understand?"

There were those in the posse who had that in mind and Brag could see that thought in Gillette's eyes.

The parties hid their horses in draws in the care of one man, sought cover on the nearest ridges, cocked their rifles and settled down to wait.

Balbo would make the first move. Moving boldly on his horse, he drew up to the cabin, dismounted and shouted Stephanic's name.

A rifle shot rang out, nicking Balbo on the left shoulder and knocking him to the ground. As he lay there, he held up one hand.

"No shooting, men!

"Stephanic, come out! You're surrounded! We don't want to kill you, but we will if you resist. I'm here to take you in as a suspect in the murders of the Blakes. Will you surrender?"

The cabin door swung open and a Winchester rifle flew through the air, landing in front of Balbo.

"I'm coming out. I'm unarmed."

Stephanic appeared at the door, hands in the air. Brag and forty-eight other men sighted down their rifles. It was all too easy, Brag thought.

Stephanic was a thin, wiry man with a heavy, black beard and shoulder-length hair pulled back and tied in a queue with a rawhide strap. He wore no hat, his bib overalls were filthy from chest to cuffs and his long-sleeve checkered shirt was torn in a dozen places. Brag could smell him from a hundred yards away.

Stephanic took three steps toward Balbo, now standing with pistol leveled, then fell on his knees and face in the dirt.

"Please, I'm sorry. Don't kill me. I didn't mean to do it," he exclaimed. A murder confession, on the spot, in front of fifty witnesses, Brag thought.

He looked at Gillette, standing twenty feet away, rifle leveled and ready.

"Don't do it, Ed!" Brag whispered.

"Boy, I sure want to. Make sure he pays, save the county a lot of money." He lowered his rifle and snarled. "Maybe the townsfolk will lynch the bastard when we get him back."

Balbo cuffed the man while others searched the cabin. "Whew! First thing we do is throw you in the nearest creek," he said.

"Nothing in here, Balbo," shouted the searchers. "But, boy, what a stench."

"Pull his personals out, any weapons, any books, pictures, mail, anything we can use as evidence, then burn the place," Balbo ordered.

The cabin went up in minutes, like a shock of wheat, leaving only glowing embers.

"Good job, men. Time to head back," Balbo declared.

"We could ride north to Gillette and catch the train at end-of-track," Gillette suggested. "It's about forty miles, half the distance. Save us a long ride back."

Balbo shook his head and laughed as he mounted a tired horse. "I like your style, Mr. Gillette. I'd have never thought of that and I'm sure the men here appreciate it."

Gillette's suggestion drew a collective "yea" from the men as they mounted up and headed north, Stephanic in the middle of the posse.

Brag rode beside Gillette as they followed the Coal Creek draw.

"Thought for sure you were going to gun him back there," he said.

Gillette looked at him and smiled. "Naw, just drawing down on him like about some other guys were doing. Just making him crap in his bibs." Brag would have been surprised by any other answer.

"My mother died three days ago," Brag said offhand.

Gillette didn't say anything for a few moments, then, "Yea, I know, Day told me. Bad luck comes in bunches out here sometimes, Brag, and you've got to be strong for it." He shook his head, bumped his horse against Brag's and squeezed his arm.

"You are one of the most likeable young hands I've known and everyone in the crew likes you, too. My regrets that your mother has passed on, that Tom and Bertha are gone, that you are not working with us anymore."

He picked the makings out of his shirt pocket and expertly rolled a cigarette, the only man Brag knew who could roll a butt in the saddle against the wind.

"I know you haven't been out here long enough to get hardened, but if your luck keeps running the way it has, you soon will," Gillette continued. "I want you back on my crew and I'm going to talk to Day when we get back to Gillette."

In Gillette, Brag was greeted like a long-lost brother. The new citizens of Gillette and the survey crew surrounded the posse as it pulled up in front of the hotel. Some were ready to lynch Stephanic on the spot.

"Caught the bastard, right?" exclaimed Mike.

"Serve him right if we hang him right here and now," echoed Joe.

"There will be none of that, men. We are taking him back to Cambria for trial," Balbo said. "He's staying overnight here and I don't want to have to put down a lynch mob, understand?" The look in his eyes was enough to cut the talk. He locked Stephanic in the town's new jail.

"Good to meet you finally, Brag," said Johnson, shaking his hand. "All I've heard the past months are how great you were out here with the crew. I only hope you're not sore at me for taking your job."

Brag sized him up. Squat and heavily built with a pale complexion and eyes squinting through spectacles, Johnson was the perfect picture of a dime-store clerk, certainly not one of a pioneer trail-blazer. He wondered how he cut such a rugged life out here on the frontier.

"Not sore, now, but there for a while I was pissed off at everybody, including you," Brag responded. "Things, though, have a way of working out and I'm sure you are happy to be out in the boondocks."

A shadow crossed Johnson face as he looked away. "No, to tell the truth, rather be back in Omaha with my folks. Didn't realize how tough it is out here, but then, it's a job. As soon as

I can I'm going to tell Day I've had it out here."

Good to hear, Brag thought.

Gillette was a neat collection of new, high-front wooden buildings, so new buffalo grass still grew in the streets. The town was named for Gillette because he and his crew, Brag included, had surveyed a shorter route which saved building thirty bridges and numerous miles. The route of the original survey party had turned south of the Rozet siding, followed Donkey Creek to the Powder River, then down Hay Creek and Wildhorse Creek. Donkey Town was started on the Continental Divide miles away, a tent town looking to sprout with the coming of the railroad. Gillette's new survey killed the town.

When Brag and the posse reached Gillette that brisk October afternoon, the town was a thriving little city, with a mayor and justice of the peace. There were the Daly brothers store, the Adams' store, the Seth Reiner store, a boarding house, the Windsor Hotel, a bank, a commissary and livery barn run by Kilpatrick Brothers and Collins, numerous cafes, seven saloons and three dance halls. The *Gillette News* was published by Judge Alden, also the justice of the peace.

The B&M built a roundhouse, depot, section house, a club house for its crews, coal and sand tipples and an eating house called, without much inspiration, the Beanery.

The town almost immediately became a railroad terminal for shipping cattle from the large ranches and herds built through the years in Crook and Weston counties.

Gillette was even more modern and progressive than Newcastle, Brag thought.

Brag unpacked his saddle bags in the club house and stood in line with the rest of the crew to take a bath. It was a bittersweet reunion, what with Tom and Bertha's murders and the death of Brag's mother, word of which had already spread through the crew.

"Sorry to hear about your mother, Brag," Joe said as he toweled off. "I know that pain. My dad died couple of months ago." He got condolences from every member of the survey party.

The town mayor, Balbo and Gillette joined Brag and the crew for supper at the Beanery that evening. Their mood had brightened and their jocular conversation soon dispelled Brag's depression.

Gillette introduced Brag to the mayor. "Brag's one solid telegrapher and not too bad a surveyor, either," Gillette noted. "We're trying to get him back on the party because we need him badly, what with all that has happened."

"And, I want badly to be back on the crew, too," Brag countered.

He knew Elly would not be happy with him back in the boondocks and gone for months on end, but he thought she would understand. In fact, she had told him on several occasions that he was becoming a bore around the house, that he was drinking too much and ignoring Jennie May. She was right, he thought.

He was floored when Day took him off the survey party for reasons Brag thought not legitimate. Elly didn't nag him about that, thank God, but he could feel a new coldness in her, something he didn't understand. Maybe it was the new baby, he didn't know. Then, the murders of Tom and Bertha and the death of Rebecca, coming as they did so close together. Maybe Gillette was right. Maybe he wasn't hard enough, man enough, to stand up to bad news, an almost daily happening here on the frontier.

Well, it was all over now. Things had been resolved. A murderer had been caught, Brag had sent off a telegram to his father and family and Gillette was stumping to get his job back. As for Elly, he'd have to work that out when he got back.

Friendly conversation and prime steaks passed around the table freely that night in the Beanery.

Then a shot rang out.

Someone had shot Stephanic dead in his cell.

On to Sheridan

The fight started in Manuel Armenta's Dance Hall and Saloon in the boom town of Sheridan. No one could recall how it got going, but Brag was the second man knocked on his butt.

It was his first fray, other than those with his brothers, and he wasn't about to lose it. He got up, drunk and half-blind, and swung at the first man he could see. It was the party's amiable hunter, Pierre, a lumbering ox of a man six feet tall and weighing a good seventeen stone. Brag's blow glanced off his shoulder and Pierre brushed him aside like a wood chip and went after bigger game.

Brag nailed the next two men square on the jaw. Probably drunker than me, he thought, as they fell face down on the wooden floor. He was getting in some good licks in what had started out as a local misunderstanding and now was a wild free-for-all. The fancy girls fled upstairs, tables, chairs and bottles flew like buckshot and windows were shattered by flying bodies.

Brag was having a grand time until the next blow fell. It wasn't his. Someone, he never saw who, laid one on his jaw and sent him tumbling through the half-doors into the snow in the dirt street. Through semi-consciousness, he heard the townsfolk yelling as they leaped up and down, thoroughly enjoying the fracas.

He staggered to his feet, his head cleared and he headed back toward the saloon. Someone grabbed him, turned him around and shoved him back through the doors. He found another face to smash, and then a pistol shot rang out.

"Enough! Enough!" the man shouted, then fired three more shots through the ceiling.

The place suddenly went quiet, except for the grunts and moans of injured men and the tinkle of glass and whiskey still flowing from dozens of broken bottles. Brag stood up, leaned against a post and wiped the blood from his nose and lips. He felt no pain.

Brag recognized the man with the pistol. It was Ben Barker, the burly chief carpenter for the B&M.

"All right, you men, get your wounded together, B&M men on this side of the room, and Dan, get your Sheep Creek tie-hacks over on this side," Barker gestured. "I don't know who started this thing, but if it's a company fight, it's over, right now!" Brag later learned that Dan was one Dan Starbird, co-owner of a sawmill and tie hack operation in the Big Horn Mountains.

The men rearranged the mess and resumed drinking, the fancy girls returned and the piano player hacked out a tune on the battered piano, as if nothing had happened. Barker and Starbird huddled with Armenta, discussed the damages and decided to split expenses. Armenta seemed satisfied, probably because he redecorated his place and cleared a few bucks to boot after every set-to like this.

Brag leaned back against the bar, wrapped his sore hand in

a bandanna and drank from the bottle. The place resembled the wreck of his life the past year of '91 and he pondered on it. He was used to bad times, all they had back on the farm. Out here on the frontier, though, seemed like hard times came in bunches and he found it difficult to handle.

After the Stephanic posse disbanded and Brag got back to Cambria, Day had orders for him to rejoin Gillette and the survey party working up near Dayton.

That wasn't the only good news.

Elly told him she was pregnant again, but suffering more than with Jennie May. She was in such a depressed mental state that Brag was truly concerned. He hugged and kissed her when he walked in the door, but that was the only affection she demonstrated toward him during the two days before he left for the field again.

"I know you are not feeling well, dear. Is there anything I can do for you, anything I can get you?" Brag asked.

"No," she said, and left it at that.

Elly knew Brag was going back before he did, a fact she learned from her father. Brag didn't tell her until later that day and when she didn't say a word, he sensed she knew it already.

"I got my job back with Gillette, isn't that great?" he said. "Apparently Day pulled some strings. Johnson obviously doesn't want the job and Gillette did a little legislating for me, too."

She just nodded and went about her business without a word.

"Look, Elly. I'm really happy we've got a new baby coming and I hope it's a boy to go along with Jennie May." He was trying to reach her, to penetrate a wall that she seemed to throw up after Jennie May was born. "I know you're hurting, maybe more so than when you carried Jennie May and I want to help."

She dropped the sewing in her lap and stared directly at him.

"The only way you can help now is to stay at home, be with me through this."

When he told her he couldn't, she exploded.

"You mean, you won't. I haven't seen you in nearly two weeks, off chasing some idiot, and before that only late at nights. Just long enough to knock me up and leave. And, even then, you come home plastered to the gills. Is that all you think of me, an occasional bed partner?"

Brag had never seen her so angry before.

"Please, honey, don't get upset, you'll hurt the baby."

"Damn the baby, damn you, damn it all!"

He tried to calm her, tried to hold her, caress her cheek, but she broke away sobbing. He felt the anger rising and then it was his turn.

"Dammit, woman, all I'm trying to do is make a living, keep our heads above water, do the right thing for both of us. This job with Gillette is the only way I know how to do that."

She slammed the bedroom door in his face.

Brag poured himself a drink, stared at the door and made a decision. He would talk to Townsend.

He hitched a ride with a miner into Newcastle, found a phone and placed the call. Townsend's pleasant voice answered.

"Mr. Townsend, I have to talk to you about Elly," Brag began.

"Is she okay? She hasn't miscarried, has she?"

"No, she's fine, Mr. Townsend. It's just that she seems to have retreated into a shell lately. We haven't been getting along well at all."

Townsend's reply was quick and calm. "Well, I'm not surprised. It runs in the family." Brag was puzzled.

Townsend went on. "You see, Brag, Jennie acted the same way with the twins. I don't know what it is with the Stockner women, they all seem to be possessed by the devil while they're pregnant. I wouldn't worry too much about it."

Brag hesitated, mulling his answer. "But, she hardly will speak to me, cries a lot and won't let me even touch her."

Townsend laughed. "I think that's the bane of all pregnant women, Brag. The way I handled Jennie was to just ignore her temper tantrums, step around them. Be considerate, express your love for Elly and just weather the storm. It will pass with the new birth.

"Of course, the difference is that I was with Jennie constantly," he continued. "We hardly ever were apart. That's not your case. You'll be in the field again and Elly may not understand that. I'll say this, however. The more she misses you, the more affectionate you'll find her, mark my word."

"Okay, Mr. Townsend, but I'll be back out in the field in two days and there's no one to look after Elly while I'm gone."

"Doesn't she have a woman friend up there? If not, try to find a midwife in town somewhere, someone who can be with her while you're gone."

Brag never thought of that. Perhaps all Elly needed, in lieu of him not being there, was a companion, someone with her constantly.

"I'll try to find someone, and thanks," he said.

"Good luck in the field, Brag."

As his luck would have it, Brag was in the field north of Sheridan when Theron Warren was born on a blustery November afternoon. Brag had found a midwife in Newcastle, so the birth was not as traumatic as Elly had predicted. Still, it would have been better for her if he had been there.

Starbird interrupted Brag's daydream.

"You're Brag Cooper, the B&M's telegrapher in these parts, right?" he said, shaking Brag's sore hand.

"I hope I didn't knock you on your ass." He laughed, bought Brag another drink and said, "I know Winfield Townsend well. He and my Omaha partner are good business friends. Heard you married his daughter?"

Brag liked the man right off. "That's right. Just had another kid last month, a boy, Theron Warren Cooper."

"That's makes two for Aletha, doesn't it?" Starbird responded. Brag was surprised.

"Hell, Townsend keeps us informed of everything that's going on along the line between Omaha and Sheridan," Starbird revealed. "My partner is Tom Hall, the postmaster in

Omaha, and he travels in the same company with Townsend and his like. They're all a bit snobby for my taste, but great folks."

Brag wanted to know more despite the man's obvious dislike for "snobs." He never looked at Townsend or any of his associates he'd met quite that way.

"You running ties for the B&M?" he asked.

"Yep, just started. Let's find an unbroken table and I'll tell you about it." He bought a bottle and Brag sat down to hear his story.

Starbird said he and Hall had a contract to provide the B&M with one-million ties by the fall of '93. He said he and John Thurston, the B&M's tie boss, had scouted out an area and set up a camp that summer of '91 on Sheep Creek on the eastern slopes of the Big Horns.

"We had a steam boiler and sawmill freighted in and our lumberjacks are already cutting timber to build the flume down the river," Starbird stated. Actually, he said, there eventually would be two operations, one to cut and mill lumber for the flume, the other to hack ties to be floated down the flume.

Then, Starbird went into a long, involved explanation of the tie hacking process, which Brag tolerated only because he had no other place to go.

"Them tie hackers are a breed apart," Starbird began. "Some of the strangest men I've ever met, but they certainly know their business."

Tie hacks generally worked in pairs with broad axes shaped and sharpened for left and right work. One hack would fell the tree, the other cleared off the branches. With his left broad axe, one hack would flatten the left side of the tree while the other flattened the other side. The bark was stripped, the log cut into eight-foot tie lengths and stamped with the hacks' brand to identify who made the tie. Tie hacks received from eight to ten cents a tie.

"Some of my men can peel off a log so neatly you'd think it was run through a planner," Starbird bragged.

After the ties were hewn, they were thrown into Freeze Out Pond near the mill, then floated down the flume to where Sheep Creek ran into the Tongue River.

"That flume is going to be the eighth wonder of the world," Starbird exclaimed. "My men are already building it, from the logging site down the canyon to the Tongue River. We'll have it finished soon. Then, we can float the ties right on down the Tongue to Dayton where your railroad will be waiting for them." He sat, back, swilled another drink and laughed.

Brag didn't want to pop his balloon, but he knew the B&M wasn't going through Dayton. Brag's survey party would stake out a new route north of Dayton in the next few days. Gillette had told him about the interesting background of the route change.

Earlier that fall, the B&M's right-of-way purchasers tried to buy forty acres on a site just across the river from Dayton. They wanted the land, owned by one Henry Baker, for a depot, switch yard and to store the ties coming down the Tongue. Baker said he didn't want to sell that small a parcel because it would break up his ranch, but that he would sell all four hundred and eighty acres.

The B&M men asked how much, and that's when Baker got greedy and doomed Dayton as a railroad town. He had been trying to sell his spread for twelve thousand dollars, but he hoped to make a killing off the B&M and retire. He told them twenty-four thousand dollars. The B&M men said *adios* and went back to Omaha.

That's when Gillette, Brag and the survey party entered the sad saga of Dayton. The right-of-way party had been fairly successful buying property on the proposed road. It would go down Goose Creek to the Tongue River then up the river valley past Dayton, where the ties would be waiting. When Perkins heard the price Baker was asking, he nixed the deal and told Gillette to survey another route.

One cold autumn morning of '92 they staked out a line across the appropriately named Five Mile Flat. It was five miles north of Dayton and bypassed the Baker spread and the disheartened townsfolk there. A new town, Ranchester, sprang up at the juncture of Five Mile Creek and the Tongue River to welcome the ties, and the railroad, with open arms.

Brag and the survey crew settled in Sheridan for their work around Ranchester.

"There's a phone call for you, Brag," yelled Carl Mikkelson. Mikkelson was the Sheridan stationmaster and Brag's boss when he was in town.

"Who the hell's calling me way out here?" Brag replied.

"Don't know, but it's a woman."

"Brag, it's Elly!" She sounded frantic. Brag held his breath.

"Oh, honey, I've got wonderful news for you. Daddy has bought land for us in Ranchester. He has timber interests up there and says the railroad is going through Ranchester soon and will be building new houses there, and we…"

He interrupted. "Wait a minute, Elly, slow down!" Her voice was bright and bubbly and he could hear the babies crying in the background. He was delighted she called.

"You want to move up here?" he asked.

"Oh, yes, Brag. I've missed you so and now we can be together. Don't you think it's grand?"

He did.

"I'm packing right now and I'll be on the next work train to Clearmont," she exclaimed. "Pick me up at the depot tomorrow afternoon. Oh, Brag, I love you so and I can't wait to see you."

Townsend was right. Elly did genuinely miss him, he could tell from her voice. He had been in the field three months now and he missed her, too.

"But, Elly, Clearmont is almost forty miles from here and I don't know if I can get off. Besides, there's no place to live up here. Ranchester is still a tent town, there are no houses there yet. I don't know if I can find a place here in Sheridan, it's so crowded."

There was silence at the other end of the line and Brag bit his tongue. He shouldn't have crushed her enthusiasm so abruptly.

But, she answered, brightly as before. "Yes, I know, Brag, but I do so want to be with you, right now. Can't you arrange something?"

Her excitement was contagious and he felt an old yearning rising in his chest.

"Okay, you come on. I'll meet you in Clearmont and we'll find someplace here, even if it's in a tent."

Jimmy hauled him to Clearmont in the company's spring wagon, talking a mile a minute about Indians, rattlesnakes and the Mississippi.

Elly looked glorious when she stepped from the train carrying a baby in each arm. Jennie May was nearly a year old, a bright, alert little girl with dark hazel eyes and shoulder-length auburn hair, a carbon copy of Elly. Theron's chubby face and brown eyes stared at him from under the blanket. "Okay, so I was half right, he's got brown eyes already," Brag chuckled.

"Here's your daddy, Jennie," Elly said as she set Jennie May down. Jennie toddled over and he picked her up. She played with his nose, his lips, stuck a finger in his eye and babbled a couple of unintelligible words. She was enchanting.

Then, he swept Elly into his arms, kissed her hard and held her tight. "I have missed you so."

She returned his kisses with her old fervor and handed him the baby. "And, so have I. It's so good to feel your arms around me again after so long."

"Mornin', Miss Cooper," Jimmy said in his best Southern manner. "We'd best be goin', there's a storm a'brewin' over the Horns." She had brought a ton of luggage which nearly filled the spring wagon.

Brag held Jennie May on his lap as they followed the line road, waving to the grading crews as they passed. Clearmont was end-of-track, but Sam Gwinn and his grading crews were only twenty miles east of Sheridan and the rail-laying crews were not far behind.

"I talked to Carl, my boss in Sheridan, and he said you and the children can stay at Ma Cornwall's Windsor Hotel right in

Sheridan," Brag revealed. "Our survey party is holed up on the Holdredge ranch north of town. We're working through Ranchester and the Montana line is not too far away, Elly."

A shadow crossed her face. "So, you won't be staying with us in Sheridan?"

"Yes, as a matter of fact, we ride into Sheridan every night and leave early every morning. That is, if we can round up the party after their nightly binges. Sheridan is a very wild town, you'll soon discover."

She looked at him and laughed. "I suppose you've done your share of that, too?"

He smiled and kissed her. "Well, yes, I put down a few, but it's mostly social drinking. I've met some of the nicest folks and I think you'll like Sheridan, it has some of the most hospitable people I've ever met."

She laughed again and squeezed his hand. It was good to see the old sparkle back in her eyes.

Ma's hotel was one of the first hotels erected at Main and Works Streets in Sheridan, already a busy town even before the railroad came. The hotel had a saloon, a dining room, a sitting room and a number of upstairs boarding rooms, some set up as suites. Ma Cornwall herself was an imposing women in her forties with a stern countenance that belied a heart of gold underneath her generous bosom. Hers was one of the pioneer families who had settled the town back in '82, when the first plat stakes were driven by Jack Dow on the original forty acres.

"Well, aren't you just the prettiest girl in town," Ma Cornwall exclaimed, embracing Jennie May as they entered the hotel lobby. Elly liked Ma right then and there.

"We are so delighted, Brag, you could bring your family up. Why, just look at them, aren't they all just the prettiest women in town? I heard the Cooper clan was just about the handsomest in these parts and now I believe it."

She nearly smothered Elly and little Theron with her embraces, then led them to their upstairs rooms. "Didn't I tell you, Elly, Ma is just great," Brag whispered.

Ma kept a neat, clean, almost antiseptic, hotel despite the dust and mud of the yet ungraveled streets. Bouquets of prairie and mountain flowers were everywhere, as was the sharp scent of mountain pine. The rooms were large, bright and airy and looked out over the town and the Big Horn Mountains less than a days' ride away.

"Can we afford this?" Elly whispered as Jimmy unloaded the baggage and Ma scurried about, pulling back curtains and filling the water basins.

He had another surprise for her. After she said she was coming, Brag made some inquiries. He knew some of his survey party stayed at various boarding houses in town, but Mike, Joe and Jerry stayed at Ma's with their families. All, of course, were upstairs, away from the ruckus and noise of the saloon and street.

"You'll get to meet some of my crew soon, honey," he revealed. "Three of them and their families live right here and you won't be so lonely anymore."

He could see Elly was happy with his arrangements. "Oh, Brag, it's just lovely. Why, it even has a separate bedroom for the children and a window view of the mountains. I couldn't ask for anything nicer, except maybe our own house."

"I think I can scrape up another crib for the baby and maybe some baby clothes, too," Ma said. "Seems like all I've done the past three months since your crew arrived was hunt down baby things. Just amazing how this town's growing, what with all you fine young folks moving in and all." She seemed to be constantly on the move and hustled out of the room with a "see you at supper" wave.

"She's marvelous," Elly exclaimed. "I'm going to like it here, Brag."

Jimmy finished carting the baggage up the stairs and stopped for a breath. "Sure do like the way you folks travel, yes sir, sure do," he gasped. "Like when I was a'tottin' stuff for my master back in 'Sippi. Say, Mr. Brag, don't you think I'd better hustle down and get some milk 'n stuff for them babies? They look mighty hungry to me."

"Not necessary, Jimmy. Mrs. Cooper brought her own milk along, see?" Brag replied. Elly had settled into a chair at the window and was nursing Theron.

"Oh, 'scuse me, sir. Almost forgot the Misses has her own supply."

"Yea, and it comes in such cute containers, right, Jimmy?"

He blushed and quickly fled the room and Brag broke up.

Elly hummed softly as she nursed Theron. Brag was more at peace than he had been in what seemed like a hundred months. She motioned for him to pull up a chair and he sat next to her at the window as a pallid winter sun set over the Big Horns.

Yes, he thought, there was a wonderful serenity here on the Wyoming high plains. He forgot the agony and frustration of the past two years and opened his mind to what might lay ahead. With '92 closing out in a few weeks, he was looking ahead to being with Elly and the children, to his work in the field with Gillette and his new-found friends and even beyond. Even the question of where they would be once the B&M hooked up with the Northern Pacific, perhaps in two more years, was not important now. What was important was that his family was with him, that he and Elly were off to a fresh, new start. Right now, it was vital that the two of them stay together, at least for a while.

Elly sighed, burped Theron and laid him in the crib. She must have been musing, too, Brag thought as he undressed. He wondered what she was thinking.

She answered quickly enough as they snuggled into bed. Their love-making was tentative for only a moment, then she reminded him that her fire had not been extinguished by a few months of abstinence.

North to the Line

Elly stared out the window at Brag riding through the snow to work and she knew he wouldn't be back for a week.

She felt the new baby kicking in her belly and was alert to a cry from the five-month-old twins, Bessie and Margaret. They were snuggled together under a blanket on the floor with Jennie May and Theron asleep on either side of them.

She looked back out the window just as Brag disappeared through the trees along the river. She was sorry for him and tears crowded her eyes. She felt the hurt in her chest again. It wasn't the baby, although she was carrying this one higher than the others.

The pain started two months before, on the day the Coopers were kicked out of Ma Cornwall's hotel. They were in hock up to their eyes with four bawling children and no place to live.

Ma Cornwall sold her hotel that summer of '94 and the new owners had called in the three thousand dollar debt against the Coopers. Ma's great, good heart had let the monthly board and room slip by for the two years the Coopers stayed. But, the new owners were adamant and, when Brag couldn't come up with the money, they found themselves in the street sitting on their baggage.

Brag could have redeemed the Ranchester property or the trust fund Townsend had set up for them, had they been there. Townsend and thousands of other businessmen had lost their savings and businesses in the financial panic of '93. The Sherman Silver Purchase Act had been passed four years before as a compromise with the free silver advocates. Its threat to the U. S. Treasury's gold reserves caused a wild panic that swept the country. President Grover Cleveland secured a repeal of the act through Congress in '93, but the damage had been done. The country was deep in depression and the Coopers, like millions of others, were hard hit.

Brag found an old, abandoned trapper's cabin a few miles south of Hardin, Montana, in the Big Horn River valley and the family moved in. It cost them nothing, which was all they could afford.

Brag blamed Elly for their plight and she, in turn, pointed a finger at him.

"You spend your money in the saloons carousing and whoring and we've got nothing!" she shouted as they trudged up to the cabin. Their argument over money had been raging for months.

"Bullshit, Elly!" he responded, shoving the children into the bleak, dark cabin. "I've never touched another woman and my carousing, as you say, was never more than a few social drinks with the men." Brag knew that was only a half-truth.

She looked around the cabin and her heart sank. It was a dilapidated one-room log structure with a crumbling stone fireplace, one battered wooden table and a few rickety chairs. The only window opened onto the river and daylight poured through holes in the wooden slat roof. Her hotel room was a palace compared to this, Elly thought, and her depression deepened.

"How about you, how about all those clothes and fancy things you've been buying all these years?" Brag countered. "You hardly ever bought clothes for the kids. Ma Cornwall provided most of them. And, how about the times she fed them out of her own kitchen? You never even had the consideration to buy food for them and never, ever paid Ma back, for anything.

"You just kept running up the bills and Ma was too kind to say anything about it," he exclaimed. He left out the fact that Elly often left the children alone to attend some sewing bee or social, relying on the wives of his friends or a saloon whore to watch over the youngsters.

"You were gone so often the kids hardly knew who their mother was," he said. "I don't know what happened, Elly, but you've gone completely sour in the past two years."

She cried then. "How about you? You came home so late and left so early that Jennie May and Theron didn't even know a man slept there, let alone their father." She had to get in the final word. "You only showed up every night to get a piece of tail, roll over and go to sleep."

"You could have said no anytime," he said and stomped out of the cabin.

Brag could understand part of her argument. For nearly two years, she and her brood had been cooped up in that small three-room suite in the hotel in Sheridan. The only place Jennie May and Theron could play was in the dirty, rat-infested lot behind the hotel. The street out front was equally dirty and infinitely more dangerous. Mike, Joe and Jerry all had children, but much older and not inclined to play with the Coopers. There were other town children, but they found their fun and games elsewhere.

Ma had suggested that Elly get away from her kids on occasion by joining a women's social circle in town. Ma would see to the children. It was an innocent enough proposal, but the deeper Elly committed to the outside socials, the more she neglected her maternal duties. She found it easy to leave the hotel for hours on end during the days, chatting and socializing. Then, the guilt began eating deep within her. Brag knew nothing of her daily sojourns, nor the guilt that tore at her, because Ma wouldn't presume to tell him and Elly never did.

The whole situation blew up one spring morning when Brag and the survey party returned early to Sheridan.

As Brag was unsaddling his horse, he saw a group of women walking down the street, their long, print skirts dragging in the dust. Elly was with them, in a new dress he'd never seen before.

He wanted to rush over, gather her in his arms and kiss her, right in front of the whole town. Then, he thought, where was she going? Where were the children? Jennie May and Theron were old enough now to pretty much fend for themselves, but the twins, Bessie and Margaret, were just toddlers and somebody must be looking after them. He hoped it was Ma or the wives of Mike, Joe or Jerry.

He decided to spend the afternoon with his men at Armenta's saloon, go back to the hotel at his regular time and see what Elly was up to. That was justified, in his own mind, but later he felt guilty he had not just gone on home.

When he walked in the door, bleary-eyed with whiskey on his breath, Elly exploded. It was the start of a quarrel which had their relationship going downhill the past two years.

The B&M Railroad was inching the last miles across south-central Montana to its historic conjunction with the Northern Pacific Railroad. Gillette told Brag he expected the rails would be down and the first train would steam into Huntley just east of Billings in October, only a month away now.

Gillette said the crew would make its final survey around Huntley to stake out the rail yards, then the long, gruelling job would be finished. A huge last-spike driving party would be held, with brass from the Burlington and the Northern Pacific and a host of other dignitaries, then Gillette would say good-bye to his survey crew.

Brag felt that destiny was deserting him. He needed a refuge to look back on all that had happened since he had left the farm, to collect his thoughts, to ponder how to make it up to Elly.

He did not tell Elly that, after the survey party was broken up, they might have to move. Where, he didn't know. That was up to Day and his superiors. He couldn't face her, so he rode into Billings that afternoon and took a room at the Northern Pacific's hotel there.

It was snowing hard when he carried a bottle of whiskey, a pitcher of cold water and some sandwiches up to his room, locking the door behind him. A third of the way through the bottle, his mind was whirling through the events that had transpired. He could see them clearly, the characters and happenings sharp and alive.

The survey party had finished its new route through Ranchester and moved steadily northwest through the late summer and fall of '94. He remembered the place names as they covered the ground, the sidings they surveyed out, the yards, the wyes so the big mallet locomotives could turn around.

The town names raced through his head—Ohlman, Parkman, Aberdeen, Wyola, Spear, Little Horn. On and on, through Benteen and Crow Agency and Dunmore, Fort Custer, Hardin and on and on, until finally the name Ranchester stuck in his head.

Ranchester sprung up like a dandelion out of necessity—the B&M needed ties. Starbird's tie mill forty miles south in the Big Horn Mountains was meeting its quota, but Starbird himself was long gone. He and his partner had gone broke hiring the hundreds of tie hacks, flume runners and river rats needed to bring the ties down the Tongue River to Ranchester. The financial hysteria of '93 and three arrests for various misdemeanors spelled the end for Starbird. He and Hall sold out to J. H. McShane and Jerry Dunley, the camp became known as the McShane Tie Company and the flow of ties continued unabated. Before they bought the tie camp, McShane and Dunley had run grading crews which did much of the line from Omaha to Sheridan and already possessed a number of strong team horses, put to good use at the tie camp.

The survey party moved inexorably north up the Little Bighorn River, past the Custer battlefield, through the Crow Indian Reservation and on to Huntley and Billings. The reservation encompassed a huge square of land in south central Montana, its southern boundary on the Wyoming border. The Crows, deadly enemies of the Sioux, had once ranged as far north as the Yellowstone River, south into central Wyoming and west into the Rockies. The Northern Cheyenne Indian reservation abutted their land to the east.

Brag remembered the day Gillette told his party about the railroad negotiating the right of way with the Crows.

"We held council at the Crow Agency with about one-hundred-thirty five Crows, Mr. McCormick, representing the railroad, and M. P. Wyman, the U. S. Indian agent," Gillette recalled. "If it wasn't that this was very serious business, it might have been one big party. The Crows, you know, are friends of us white-eyes and fought with us against the Sioux."

The Burlington formed another railroad, the Big Horn Southern, to purchase the right of way from the Montana-Wyoming border to Hardin, Gillette said. "The Burlington built the line, about one-hundred-seven miles, and bought the Southern after the work was done," he laughed.

"Well, anyway, Wyman spoke for the government and McCormick for the railroad and those Indians sure had a lot to say. The council lasted all day because each and every one of those Indians got up and spoke his piece."

The Crows asked questions, made some demands and there were some long orations, Gillette recalled with a laugh. "They are so primitive and innocent, yet they asked some sharp questions and got exactly what they wanted from the railroad."

Wyman spoke first, illustrating the advantages the Crows

would have with the railroad across their lands.

"Now, you are plagued with large wagon trains from Wyoming to Custer Station, which destroy large amounts of fencing on your farms and ruin your hay ground. They steal your horses, plows, wagons and you don't know where these things go. It is for you to say what is in your best interest.

"But, the railroad will not steal from you and will pay you for what they get. I want all of you to get up and talk. One Indian has as much right to talk as the other."

And, talk they did.

Medicine Crow spoke to his tribe at length, then turned to McCormick. "If you kill any of our cattle pay us in a month and the same with the horses. When we ship hay we want big prices for it. We want the Great Father to take care of us and treat us well when the railroad comes."

Then, almost before the council got going, Medicine Crow conceded the right-of-way. "I want to give a right-of-way for forty steps or twenty steps on each side of the road bed." Twenty steps was agreed upon.

Old Dog wanted to know how much the railroad would pay when it crossed his allotted land and how much damage money he would get. McCormick assured him that he and the railroad agent would inspect their property, discuss the matter and pay according to the damages.

"The Great Father will see that none of you are cheated," McCormick declared. "We will pay one dollar and twenty-five cents per acre for the unalloted land." Spotted Horse wanted to know how big an acre was and McCormick explained.

Spotted Horse asked three dollars an acre and a fence on each side of the railroad "so that you won't kill any of our horses or cattle."

"Whites talk good to Crows and we believe them," he continued, "but lots of things they say they don't do."

Spotted Horse was just getting started, Gillette recalled.

"We have coal and load it on the cars and get money for it. We want to ship baled hay and get money for it. We want fifty cents for each tie the Crows cut and deliver to you. If everything is not as represented, I want to go and see the Great Father and talk with him."

Bull Goes Hunting then spoke, "I was the first to build a house, the first farmer, the first that got wagons. You don't eat flour or baking powder unless it is mixed, or don't drink coffee without sugar, or bacon with something else with it. Pay us for our land before you build the road so our people can get something to eat."

Gillette said that from then on the council took on an air of great poignancy.

"We are all crowded in a bunch now, we've given away lots of land," Pretty Eagle stood up and said. "We have told you to put the railroad through our land, but give us a little more than it is worth."

Chief of the Crows, Plenty Coups was forceful. "The cars run over six horses belonging to Wolf and he has never been paid for them. I feel bad about selling our land and about the price, I did not get enough for it. It was big piece of land, lots of it. When the railroad is through and a man and his wife go to ride and the conductor puts him off and we hold on to him and both of us fall off and get killed, don't get mad."

Darkness had settled, the fire was burning low and the party sat in rapt attention as Gillette finished his recounting of the event.

"Then, it was time to make a deal," he said, "and the Crows bargained hard."

"We want to agree for the price to be paid to you for the land not allotted to any of you at one dollar and twenty-five cents," McCormick began. Spotted Horse wanted three dollars. "That is too much. All the land from the Little Horn to the line is not worth much. I tell you that all the Indians can ride our road.

"Now, I will pay you two dollars per acre for your tribal lands unalloted. Those Indians who are allotted, they will be dealt with separately.

"All in favor of two dollars stand up in your place."

Spotted Horse held up his hand. "I want three dollars for the land not yet allotted."

McCormick reluctantly agreed. "All right, all who are in favor, stand up."

All one-hundred and thirty-five Crows arose.

"Then it was all just a matter of getting their X's on the paper," Gillette concluded.

Brag poured the last drink from the bottle and flopped back on the bed, his head spinning. Gillette's tale about the Crows was the one bright spot in all his long, dreary days in the field.

A pounding on the door jolted Brag out of a deep, whiskey sleep the next morning. It was Jimmy.

"Get up, Mr. Cooper, there's been a terrible accident down at Parkman and they need every man!" he shouted breathlessly. "We gotta git you to the depot 'cause the train's a'leaving real soon."

Brag staggered from the bed, unable just yet to comprehend the situation.

"An accident? What happened?"

"Dere's been a train accident, that's all I know, Mr. Cooper. C'mon now, we gotta git goin.'"

Gillette, the crew and about one hundred other railroad workers were already on the six-car work train when Brag climbed aboard. The big locomotive spun its wheels on the icy rails, found traction and moved out. The sun was just breaking the eastern horizon.

"We've had a derailment between Pass City and Parkman, a loco and six stock cars over the side, cattle all over the hills," Gillette explained. "We have to clear the line, of course, and it won't be easy."

Brag knew the area. The survey party had struggled through snow so deep there that Joe and Brag had to break trail for the horses and pack mules. The rails climbed steadily from Ranchester north into the Big Horn range, across the border and through the Crow reservation. Trains of more than six cars needed big helper mallet locos to accomplish the grade to

Parkman, more than one thousand three hundred feet high. Parkman was one-hundred-eighteen miles south of Billings. It had a depot, stock yards, a grain elevator, a siding and an engine wye. The whole valley was prone to avalanches after heavy snowfall.

"We don't know if anyone was killed because it happened sometime during the night and nobody has gotten to the wreck yet," Gillette said. "I know, though, we'll have our hands full down there."

Three hours later their train pulled to a stop two miles north of Parkman and the crew alighted to survey the wreck.

Steam and smoke were still pouring from one engine, off the rails and half-buried in the snow on its side, only yards from a six-hundred foot drop-off. The helper engine was still on the tracks. There was no sign of the six stock cars that should have been coupled between the two locos. What appeared to be about one hundred confused cattle stood along the tracks.

"Everybody's okay, we're all okay!" yelled one of the men as the rescue crew ran up to the wreck. "The engineer, Old Jeb, is hurt bad, though, and needs help." The man was Bob Jefferson, engineer on the helper loco.

"Where's the rest of the stock?" Brag asked.

"Over the side, mister. All six cars. I don't think any of them made it." He wiped the blood from a small cut on his cheek with a shaking hand, his eyes wide with fear.

"Settle down, Bob, settle down," Gillette said calmly. He took a small flask from his pocket. "Here, take a big swill, it'll settle you down. Now, what happened?"

Jefferson took a long drink, wiped his face with a dirty bandanna and explained. "We don't know just yet, but it looks like something ripped the ties loose on that section of track there. It was dark and we didn't see it in time." He pointed toward the overturned loco.

"We've found it," yelled one of the men.

They hurried up the track a few yards and looked down at the cause of the wreck. The roadbed had shifted, causing a kink in the rails and spreading them just enough to derail the train. No one could figure out what caused the shift.

The sun had breached the eastern peaks and its golden fingers walked across the valley floor a thousand feet below.

The men stared into the depths. Hundreds of bloody cattle carcasses lay all along the descending slope and the stock cars could be seen far below, scattered like kindling wood all over the valley floor.

"Jesus!" Gillette exclaimed. "Look's like we've lost a whole herd!"

The first thing they had to do was send a man hiking down to Parkman to wire Ranchester for a railroad crane to lift the loco. Brag volunteered, but Gillette wanted him around. He sent another man, then got the crew working to repair the rails and roadbed. He also appointed a dozen men to round up the stock and herd it down to the Parkman pens.

They had hardly moved fifteen yards when a strange sound like summer thunder rose from far above them.

"Avalanche!" Gillette cried, pointing up the mountainside.

"Avalanche!" echoed Brag.

A huge, white cloud rolled down the mountain toward them, towering hundreds of feet above and boiling like an angry snow god. Cut loose from the flanks of the mountain by the sun's warmth, a million tons of snow crashed down toward the train, carrying rocks and trees in its wake. The men stared helplessly as the white maelstrom thundered toward them.

"Get under the cars! Under the cars!" one of the men screamed. The men scrambled to find cover, some under the cars, others into crevices of boulders. Brag dove under a huge boulder anchored to the mountain side of the track.

It did no good.

The avalanche ripped the entire train from the tracks and flung it tumbling down the escarpment into the valley below. It was as if a moody boy, unhappy with his toy, had swatted it aside. The work locomotive exploded halfway down the slope, killing Jeb and the fireman, then tumbled into the creek, a steaming pile of junk.

The six work cars cut a swath through the pines, bouncing over stumps and granite boulders before crashing on the valley floor in a jumble of shredded lumber. Splintered trees pierced the cars like sword thrusts, bringing instant and horrible death to those men who unfortunately chose that escape. The rumble echoed up and down the valley, then all was quiet.

Brag was buried face down in the snow gasping for breath. He struggled to clear the heavy snow from his body, stood dizzily to his feet and looked around. Snow still whirled in the air about him and nothing stirred in the deathly silence.

Then, men began to appear, but only along the depression between the mountain and the tracks. Those who dove into those crevices, including Brag, escaped the full fury of the avalanche.

"Hey, hey, anybody out there?" a man shouted. More shouts answered him and in minutes about seventy men had gathered on the tracks. Gillette, most of his survey party and Bob Jefferson had survived. The rest, including Joe and Jerry of the survey party, apparently were dead, swept over the precipice.

Many of the survivors stared wide-eyed at the scene, dazed and uncomprehending. Others fell on their knees and cried.

Gillette jarred them out of their shock.

"All right, okay, men, we've got to search for survivors," he yelled. "You men, get down there along the bank and see what you can find."

The powder snow was waist deep along the tracks, where there had been none at all only moments before. It was even deeper on the valley side of the tracks and the men struggled to reach the edge.

Brag looked down the slope. Bodies were everywhere, lying at grotesque angles and marked by splotches of blood-soaked snow. He could see more bodies farther down the slope, some dangling in the trees. Some of the cars were still clinging to the precipice, shattered lumber partially covered.

Here and there, the white, stiff legs of cattle showed above the snow.

"My God, they're all dead!" he shouted. "Joe, Jerry, where are you? Can you hear me?"

A muffled cry came from beneath one of the cars about a hundred feet down the slope.

"Get me out of here! Please, somebody, help me!"

Brag fought through the drifts, tore frantically at the boards and uncovered its source. It was Joe. Brag pawed frantically at the snow until he uncovered his face.

"My God, what happened?" Joe said through cold, blue lips.

"An avalanche, Joe. Swept us right off the tracks."

"Jerry, where's Jerry? He was with me when we dove for cover!"

Brag looked around and suddenly spotted an arm sticking up through the snow only yards away. He quickly uncovered the man's face. It was Jerry, but he wasn't breathing. Brag slapped his face, beat on his chest and almost instantly Jerry sucked in a breath, coughed, then started breathing.

"It's okay, Jerry, we've got you now," Brag said calmly. "We've got you safe now."

Brag could feel the warmth returning to Jerry's bloodless face, but he shook him several more times to make sure. Joe had recovered enough to join Brag and the two of them got Jerry to his feet.

As they scrambled up the slope toward the tracks, Brag stumbled over a body and screamed.

"What's wrong?" Jerry yelled.

"It's a body and it doesn't have any head," Brag responded as he fought back the urge to vomit.

"Did you find anybody?" Gillette shouted.

"Joe and Jerry! They made it!" Brag responded.

Jefferson and the last group of men returned from their search.

"I think they are all dead down here," Jefferson said, "but it's hard to tell. We can't get very far down the slope, it's too steep."

Gillette stared at the ground as the men gathered around, exhausted from their futile search. Nobody said a word as they stood, heads hung, somberly wondering if maybe somebody was still alive down there. All were stunned and bewildered by the sudden turn of events. One moment, they were busy clearing the wreck, and the next second, all was swept away. There was nothing left. It was a double disaster they could not comprehend.

As if to mock the survivors, the sun broke through and it was clear, cold and beautiful.

"There is absolutely no way to get down the slope or into the valley," Jefferson stammered, fumbling for the words. "They are all dead, or soon will be, and there's nothing any of us can do. Dammit! Damn it all!"

Gillette put his arm around Jefferson's shoulders, looked at the men and made the final decision. "Okay, gather up what gear you can find and we'll hike on down to Parkman. It's the only thing left to do."

Brag took one last look at the scene and knew it would forever be seared into his mind.

The men trudged silently through the snow when, suddenly, the lowing of cattle could be heard around the bend. Four bovine survivors stood on the tracks, heads low, eyes wide with fear.

Brag laughed. "I'll be damned. Those steers have nine lives."

The men laughed, too, but each knew in his own heart fate had decreed a reprieve in their lives.

The Final Rail

The last spike in the last rail to Huntley was driven on the afternoon of October 3, 1894. The celebration that followed was one townsfolk from Omaha to Oregon would talk about for years.

Brag stood with his arm around Elly, highballs in their hands, and watched the most glorious celebration in their lives unfold at the Sheridan Inn.

Last-spike parties had been going on for two days, in Billings and Huntley, and every whistle stop along the line that had a saloon and railroad men and women to fill it.

"Oh, it's so wonderful, just so wonderful!" Elly exclaimed, snuggling closer to Brag.

"You want to dance?" he asked.

They moved onto the crowded, oak floor and eased into a

waltz. It had been years since they had danced together, eons ago at their wedding in Crawford. Brag pulled her close, enjoying the warmth and curves of her body. It was like old times again.

They made a handsome couple, he thought, Elly in her flowing gown and flowered bonnet, he in the only suit he owned. Yet, they were only minor stars in a galaxy of bright suns that flowed around them.

Burlington's president, Charles E. Perkins, nodded and said hello as he danced past with his wife. George Holdrege, Burlington's general manager, swept past and tapped Brag affectionately on the shoulder. Buffalo Bill Cody held court with his tall tales at the bar, built in England of oak and mahogany and shipped all the way from Britain

Generals were everywhere, surrounded by lesser ranks, senators, congressmen and influential ranch owners. Minor and major politicians of every leaning and party crowded around the three native cobblestone fireplaces and discussed, what else, politics. Beautiful women were everywhere, hanging on the arms of powerful men. The town's many fancy ladies giggled and gawked, ignored for the most part except by lusty wranglers, miners and loggers.

Jennie and Winfield Scott Townsend fit so well into the crowd of high-powered socialites.

"It's so good to see you two together again," Jennie chimed as they danced. "I know you all have been at odds for so long, but you seem to have weathered the storm." She was always smiling, no matter what the situation, and it pleased Brag to see her again.

"Do you see who's over at the bar, Mother? It's Mr. Perkins and he even said hello to us," Elly chimed brightly.

"Yes, and I see Gillette over there, too. I'll have to shake his hand for a job well done," Townsend said.

The music changed to the Baltimore polka and Brag begged out. "What, you've forgotten how to polka?" Elly joked as they fled the dance floor. She was enjoying this so immensely that Brag swept her into his arms and kissed her.

"Oh, right here in front of the generals?" she cooed.

He laughed and downed his second Wyoming Slug, a mind-blasting mix of champagne and whiskey. She pressed his arm. "Careful, or you won't be able to ride tonight." It was a not so subtle hint of the bed pleasures they had happily resumed.

He kissed her cheek and said, "You've learned to accept my carousing, then?"

She looked up at him and smiled. "I've learned to accept a lot from you, Brag, dearest."

Gillette and his party found their way across the dance floor, pulled up abruptly in front of Brag and saluted.

"I salute you, Mr. Brag Cooper, for a job well and truly done." He paused, then saluted Elly. "And, to you Mrs. Cooper, I salute you a thousand thousand times for keeping this man on track, so to speak." They laughed, embraced, Gillette kissed Elly and they drank down more Slugs.

They were all here, Brag's entire survey crew, except for Jimmy. He and the other Negroes, things as they were, were outside enjoying their separate party.

"I hope our kids are staying sober," Jerry said. Brag introduced him to Elly, thankful he had shed the mule smell. "Your gang is over there by the fireplace with ours. Let's hope they let the roving barmaids go by without taking something."

Brag chuckled and Elly looked concerned. "Oh, Jerry, do you think they would do something like that?"

Gillette cut in. "Well, Elly, I would suspect they would, giving who their fathers are." They all broke up laughing.

All five of the Cooper children, plus the forty or so from other families, were being cared for by hired sitters in the inn's spacious lodge room. Brag could see into the room and occasionally got a glimpse of Jennie May and Theron cavorting with the other youngsters. It was obvious they were enjoying their time away from their parents.

The Wyoming Slugs were beginning to work. Gillette swept Elly onto the dance floor, followed in turn by Jerry, Joe and Mike. Brag danced with their wives.

Suddenly, Brag spotted a familiar face. It was Justin Dvorak, the misplaced homesteader. He spotted Brag at the same time and ambled over.

"Well, Mr. Dvorak, seems you didn't make it to the Tetons, after all."

Dvorak shook his hand, hefted his drink in a toast and swallowed it in one gulp. He was obviously feeling no pain.

"Seems that way, Mr. Cooper," he replied, his words a slur. "I got started the very day I saw you, but I got sidetracked by a pretty girl here in this evil town." He swept another drink off the silver tray as it went by. "She was so pretty, why she put the Tetons to shame. In fact, Mr. Cooper, I married her and settled down right here. I work in the commissary now."

Brag smiled as Dvorak tottered off toward his beautiful, young lady.

His world had come full circle, Brag thought, as he watched Elly and Gillette whirl through a society minuet.

From day one at Crawford, so many eons ago, Brag and his party had charted four hundred miles of wild Wyoming Territory. He felt he knew every rock, tree, creek and arroyo between Crawford and Billings, every town that sprang up and became a ghost as people passed it by, every person he'd ever met along the way. There were so many of them, and he recalled every name, every face.

They marched through his mind in one, long parade as he stared blankly at the dancers. Rebecca's face came first and a pang went through his heart.

Then came his brothers and sisters, John Berry and his father. The kaleidoscope of faces continued. Jedediah Smith, Terrance Day, Edward Gillette, Tom Blake, Pierre, the Townsends and even Judy, the party's camp dog, who died one day of old age and was buried in her own tiny plot of prairie. The parade was double-timing now—Hunter, Perkins, Terrell, Balbo, Stephanic and on and on.

Suddenly, it stopped and five smiling, pretty faces appeared on his mind's screen, Jennie May and Theron, the baby faces of the twins, Bessie and Margaret, and the tiny one of baby Gladys. He cringed. He knew Jennie May and Theron more intimately and warmly, for they were old enough to play with, to joke with, to rough-house with and to comprehend their world. Bessie and Margaret were still toddlers and Gladys was a babe-in-arms, barely able to see, let alone grasp anything but his fingers.

He drew Elly closer, coming back suddenly to reality. She looked up at him and smiled. "You've been day-dreaming again, Brag," she whispered.

"Yes, about you and the children. I just feel so thankful you are here beside me. I find it so wonderful that you are still here, that you have put up with me for so long." He took a deep breath and downed his drink.

Elly pressed his hand to her cheek. "Let's dance again, I want to be close to you, forever."

The party reached a summit about midnight when Perkins and Holdrege held their joined hands aloft and shouted, "Ladies and gentlemen, here's a golden copy of the last spike which will be enshrined in Billings. Now, let the party begin!"

They had ample reason to celebrate.

The Burlington was now an integral part of the Northern Pacific network that could lay claim to a railroad freeway from Minneapolis-St. Paul west to the salty surf coasts of Oregon and California and south to the steamy swamps of Mississippi. Millions of ranchers, farmers, settlers, shysters, cattle barons and plain folk were to ride the iron horse west. They owed their lives and livelihood to Gillette's survey parties, the Kilpatrick Brothers and Collins' grading crews, and the Irish, Italians, Swedes, Chinese and other nationals who splattered sweat, blood and tears onto the iron rails.

It took thousands of men five tortuous years to move tons of unyielding earth, hack out thirteen million ties, tear their guts to hoist nine hundred-pound iron rails and strain their backs to pound home millions of spikes. It was unrelenting work for pennies a day, through withering heat, numbing blizzards, along buffalo and stage trails and through huge mountains, scraping, clawing, fighting for every inch of roadbed.

Death was never more than a heartbeat away. A misdirected axe, an unseen rattlesnake, a miss-timed powder fuse or a slip while coupling cars snuffed out many a life. Child birthing was too often deadly, gunslingers and outlaws abounded and murder was a common reducer of the frontier population.

White man had come to these parts after the dinosaur, the buffalo and the Indian. Then came the Spaniards and the American expeditions, then the mountain man, the trapper, the wagon trains and the settlers. All left their mark on the landscape.

None, however, touched the earth so fundamentally, so deeply and so forcefully as the railroad man. He literally carved his way into the land, and history, with iron blade, mules, black powder and muscle.

The land of the Golden West and its people, from East and West and far off foreign lands, were never again the same.

It was a magic moment in history.